Detective Armando Ramirez

and

The Iberico Ham Murder

Mary L Walsh

Published by New Generation Publishing in 2022

Copyright © Mary L Walsh 2022

First Edition

The author asserts the moral right under the Copyright, Designs and Patents Act 1988 to be identified as the author of this work.

All Rights reserved. No part of this publication may be reproduced, stored in a retrieval system or transmitted, in any form or by any means without the prior consent of the author, nor be otherwise circulated in any form of binding or cover other than that which it is published and without a similar condition being imposed on the subsequent purchaser.

ISBN
	Paperback	978-1-80369-316-3
	Ebook	978-1-80369-317-0

www.newgeneration-publishing.com

New Generation Publishing

WHAT'S YOUR STORY?

This book was published through
The Book Challenge Competition part of
The London Borough of Barking and Dagenham
Pen to Print Creative Writing Programme.

Pen to Print is funded by Arts Council, England
as a National Portfolio Organisation.

WHAT'S YOUR STORY?

Connect with Pen to Print
Email: pentoprint@lbbd.gov.uk
Web: pentoprint.org

Acknowledgments

I would love to dedicate this book to my husband Denis, for putting up with all the times I neglected him for Detective Armando Ramirez. Without his help and support I would never have finished.

I would like to thank Barbara Nadal for being a fantastic mentor and supporter during the writing of this book.

Mary Ellingford for being my grammar and sense editor and all-round proof-reader and helper. Thank you so much Mary.

Thanks to my children and grandchildren for extra support and fun times to distract me.

And to my friends who have waited patiently for this book's publication.

There are so many other people that have supported my journey in writing, Claire Steele, Carole Pluckrose, Love Letters to the World and Anna Robinson, Ian Ayris and the Pen to Print Team.

Chapter 1

In her final seconds as she felt her body fly free of the balcony and plummet to the alley below, the killer's flint-like face was reflected in Maisie Bright's eyes. A fleeting vision of her mum's smile flashed across her brainwaves, then darkness came. She lay, her body awaiting discovery in the shaded, whitewashed, cobbled backstreet. Soon insects and vermin would begin their work of clearing away the debris.

Sofia Verano Ortiz stepped out of the holiday apartment, her white clogs slapping on the marble tiled hallway. It was her last job of the morning. She pinned the stray hair that was irritating her eyelid back into the side of her head, retied the ponytail at the back with a band. She was hot and tired. Cleaning apartment D3 had taken longer than she expected. She had nearly tripped on a striped cushion in the doorway, drawers had been pulled open with their contents spilling out. The sofa in the living room had been moved, and the mattress lay awkwardly to one side exposing the skeletal wooden slats below.

Sofia was used to the mess people left in their apartments and sighed at the thought of the extra time it would take to clean. Then she would have to go to the property office, hand in the keys and drop off the laundry, go to the supermarket, pick up her children from school, prepare dinner for them all and take some to her mother-in-law.

She took her bucket filled with soapy grey water to the alley at the back of the apartment block, these days it seemed to be heavier than ever, and with her mind on her seemingly endless list of chores, she emptied its contents into the drain. As the last of the water drained away, she noticed a green shoe, heel pointing skywards on the ground a little way ahead, just in front of the large blue dumpster.

She went a little closer and behind the dumpster she saw a foot, toes outstretched then the rest of a woman's body. Sofia dropped the empty bucket which echoed its way across the pavement and ran shouting "Policia!" and "Ayuda!" until she crashed unceremoniously into retired mayor, Senor Lopez, who was out for his daily walk. He was unused to being accosted by hysterical females and let out a loud "humph" as she barrelled into his chest. After understanding Sofia's faltering explanation, he called the police and helped her to the café, just round the corner, in the Plaza de Olvida.

The sun dripped fat and lazy on the roof tops of the small Spanish town of Nerja. Blissfully unaware of the demise of the young woman in the alley. Some inhabitants fled into the dry dimly lit shade to escape the heat and take solace in a cool cerveza. Others leapt into the soaring oven of the day to lay corpse-like on striped beach towels and be cooked by the sun's rays.

The old people of the town kept to their routines: cleaning, shopping, soothing crying grandchildren or sitting bird-like on one of the many benches with their amigos pecking over the news and retreating inside for lunch.

Once the day's heat had reached its peak the town quietened in the lazy hush of the old-fashioned siesta.

Senor Lopez then began to organise the area by asking two local ladies, Senoras Gomez and Molinera, who were chatting in the doorway of Senora Molinera's house, to keep everyone out of the alley.

Even though he had retired, the former mayor always dressed impeccably. He liked to keep up the high standards of dress he had maintained whilst Mayor of the town. He knew that a local police officer, would be first to arrive at the scene, but he also expected the National Police from Malaga would follow to investigate this serious incident.

He was confident that the formidable ladies, Senoras Gomez and Molinera would be up to the task of keeping people away from the alley. He had already heard Senora Molinera chastising the local restaurant owner for placing his café tables too close to her front door. He was sure that Antoni wouldn't make that mistake again. By the time Senora Molinera had finished her tirade a crowd had gathered to witness Antoni's embarrassment and he fled to the interior of his restaurant with her words resounding in his ears.

Officer Pedro Dominguez approached the former mayor as soon as he arrived and understood the situation and all the measures that Senor Lopez had put in place. He had brought some Police Tape with him ready to seal off the area.

Pedro Dominguez had been born and brought up in Nerja and had joined the local police after finishing college, he was employed by the town hall. He had passed the selection process easily, he came from a good honest family and although he had joined in the usual harmless pranks as a teenager he had never been in any serious trouble. He was responsible for enforcing local laws and registering lost property. He had the power of arrest, but annoyingly he had to hand most cases to the National Police, who were responsible for crimes committed in towns and cities.

"No doubt that Arab, Sergeant El Baz, would be here soon, strutting around like he owned the place with women fawning over him." He thought. "While I, a Spaniard, am relegated to simple guard duty!"

This thought had pervaded Officer Dominguez' mind for a while now and although he loved the town, he felt he should be earning more and getting more recognition from the job.

He had heard that foreigners were taking jobs for less pay and putting decent Spaniards out of work! He also wished the National Police didn't always snatch the glory so that he could get a promotion, the extra money was needed now he was a husband and father.

The phone had rung that morning, he had been annoyed because it was supposed to be his day off. He took the call telling him to go to the Plaza de Olvida. A body had been found. He had left his wife Lorena grumbling about their never spending time together and kissed his little daughter, Angelina, then taking a piece of toast with him went to do his job.

"Thank you, ladies, for keeping the alley clear, I have tape now." He brandished the blue and white tape before them.

"I'll just go and tape off the other end of the alley and make sure it's all secure and then you can carry on with your morning." He smiled at Berta, he remembered her from when he was at school.

"Yes, of course. We are glad to help, aren't we Marguerite?" Berta nudged her friend's arm.

"Oh yes, of course." Marguerite agreed

Finally, when the scene was sealed off Officer Dominguez thanked the ladies once more, brushed some invisible crumbs from the front of his uniform, leaned against a pillar of the café and waited for the National Police to arrive.

Senora Gomez raised her chin in the direction of the body in the alley,

"Poor woman, I wonder what led her to such an awful death?"

"Who knows," replied Senora Molinera. "Such a terrible thing. I read about terrible things happening every day in the papers, but to think such a tragedy has come to our town, it's awful"

Chapter 2

Officer Armando Ramirez, a detective in the National Police, had taken the call about the discovery of a female body in Nerja while he was driving to work at police headquarters in Malaga. He had got up early and gone for a run before returning home to his small but perfectly tidy apartment to shower and don his working clothes, grey shirt and black trousers. He was always early for his shift even though he knew that the hours could be unpredictable. He immediately turned the car north to the motorway and headed east along the A7 to Nerja. There was little traffic as he drove out of Malaga. The sea appeared to his left between the hills the almond tree farms shimmering in the sunlight. The tunnels along the route could be treacherous and there had been many accidents. He hoped the journey would take about 45 minutes if there were no holdups.

From the little he knew, a woman's body had been found in an alley in Nerja. Maybe it was an accident, but it could be something more sinister. It was his job to find out. He had always felt the job was part of him, that it defined him, especially at the beginning of a new investigation.

When Armando arrived on the scene Officer Dominguez greeted him.

"Detective Ramirez, I'm glad it is you. I have not seen you in a while."

"Crime in Malaga has kept me busy Pedro, to be called to Nerja is unusual. What can you tell me?"

"A woman's body was found by Sofia Ortiz; she is in the café there." Pedro lifted his chin in the direction of Antoni's Café which was already filling with lunchtime customers.

"She is the cleaner for the apartments above the place where the body was found. She is a very hard-working woman with a large family. She was very shocked as you can imagine."

"Thanks Pedro, I will go and talk to her"

"The forensic team has arrived too." called Pedro as Armando walked away. "Also, Senor Lopez wants a word with you."

Senor Lopez had been a civil servant for many years including three terms as Mayor of the town, during which time he had tried to contribute to the improvement of quality of life for the inhabitants and making Nerja a town of opportunities. He was proud of Nerja and loved it's mix of tourists and locals. He loved the way families had lived in the town all their lives, sending their children to local schools and working in the many different businesses. It had remained for the most part, a Spanish working town but at the same time offered a beautiful backdrop of traditional whitewashed cobbled streets for tourists to meander through while they made their way to the Balcon de Europa and the sea. This sort of town was unique in the Spanish Costas in that many resorts shut down for the winter months leaving properties empty and restaurants and shops closed, creating a ghost town. Nerja was busy for twelve months of the year and many elderly visitors came from the UK to escape the British winter. He was upset at this incident and worried about the effect this news could have on the local businesses. Would people be put off visiting? It was bad enough with the slow recovery from recession causing all sorts of uncertainty and slowing the previously thriving property market, but a scandal in his town could be the tipping point. He also worried about the current mayor, Senor Esteban, who although he had been a counsellor for a few years had been plagued by rumours about his integrity however, nothing concrete had ever emerged. Senor Lopez made a mental note to go and see him. The last time they had met he got the distinct impression that he wanted no help or advice and was less than pleased at the suggestion that he needed it. He had put those bad manners down to nerves about making a good impression, however, he knew that there were always people who wanted to take advantage of the mayor and his position in the town, Senor Lopez had always made sure his business dealings were transparent so that no accusations of corruption could be made. It had not been easy at times.

Armando soon found Sofia who was still sniffling into a hankie and sipping a rather large coffee into which Antoni had poured a generous shot of Juan Carlos III brandy.

"Señora Ortiz, Hello, I'm Officer Ramirez of the Policia Nacional, I would like to ask you some questions if you feel able."

"I don't think I can tell you much, Officer." replied Senora Ortiz shakily.

"Please, take your time, just tell me all you saw." Sofia felt calmer already, the brandy was doing an excellent job, this policeman seemed very patient and understanding, not to mention good looking, she thought.

"I was just finishing up for the morning. The last apartment was very messy and so it took me longer than usual. I always empty the dirty water straight into the drain in the alley, it means I don't have to rewash the sink in the apartment building. Then I saw the shoe lying there and I thought it looked odd, so I went closer and that's when I saw…" Sofia began to cry once more.

Armando could see she was in shock but wanted to make sure she had told him everything.

"I won't keep you much longer Sofia. When you went into the alley did you see anyone else?"

"No Officer, there was no one around. I work for the agency in Calle Rodrigo Acosta, Gabriella is so good to me and understands if I have to change shifts because of the children or my mother-in-law. I also work later at the school cleaning. So, you see I have much to think about, my children, the shopping, the cooking, and looking after my mother-in-law. I barely have time to brush my hair in the mornings! I don't think there was anyone else, but as I told you, I wasn't paying much attention. As soon as I saw the body I ran for help and bumped into Senor Lopez and he called you. I'm sorry I can't tell you more." Sofia finally took a breath and folded her hands in her lap.

"Thank you, Sofia, if you think of anything at all, no matter how small please contact me. Here is my card." Armando handed her the small white card embossed with the logo of the National Police.

"Is someone coming to take you home?" he asked

"Oh yes, my husband, Sebastien, is coming, Senora Gomez telephoned him."

"Buenos Dias officer." Senora Marguerite Gomez took in the figure of the national police officer appreciatively. He was tall and had dark hair in a neat crew cut. His eyes were brown and looked at her with a steady gaze, there was nothing hidden in that look Marguerite thought, honest as the day is long.

Marguerite sighed as she thought of her younger days in Nerja, after she had recovered and before she became an invisible older woman. She was snapped out of her reverie by her friend Senora Berta Molinera.

"Marguerite, pay attention, the police officer is talking to you."

"My name is Armando Ramirez; I'm a detective with the National Police. I would like to ask you some questions if I may?"

"Oh! I'm sorry officer, how can I help you?"

"Did you see anything unusual this morning, Senora Gomez?"

"No Officer Ramirez," she said squinting at his warrant card, "I only knew when Senor Lopez asked my friend Senora Molinera and I to keep everyone away from the alley and the unfortunate woman until the Police came."

Armando waited, he knew the value of silence and giving people time to speak. It had been one of the first lessons he had learned upon leaving the academy. He'd questioned a witness about a robbery but not thought them important enough to waste his time, and so rushed through his questions. Later it transpired that the man had vital information about the crime that led to several arrests. He remembered the lecture his boss had given him afterwards he learned that sometimes the smallest detail could lead to the case being solved.

"You didn't hear anything last night or early this morning, Senora Molinera?"

"No" Berta replied tutting "Only the noise of that café next to my house, such a nuisance"

"And you Senora Gomez?"

"I'm afraid I cannot tell you more than I have Officer, I live on the Carabeo, two streets away so I didn't see or hear anything." Marguerite Gomez replied, "Do you know what happened Officer?"

"Not yet ladies. Thank you for your help though. If you hear or think of anything else, then please do not hesitate to call me on this number." With that he handed each of them his card, then went back to the alley and the forensic team to look more closely at the scene.

Chapter 3

Karim El Baz, his colleague from the department, suddenly appeared at Armando's side.

"Hey boss, I asked around to see if anyone witnessed anything, no information so far but I have only asked the people hanging around." he said with a shrug of his shoulders. "I think we should check the building, we may find someone who heard something. I'll take Diaz and Alvarez with me."

"Thanks Karim, ask the shop owners on Los Huertas if they noticed anyone hanging around. I will meet you later back at the station. Will you set up an incident room for us? Ring me if you find anything significant, you know our boss is going to be breathing down our necks to solve this quickly. I'm going to talk to the forensic team then head over to the agency."

Karim had come to Spain from Iran after Iraq had invaded, a war which led to the deaths of 500,000 soldiers in total. He was a child refugee and travelled with his mother and sister to escape the conflict. His father hadn't been lucky enough to escape with them and had become one of the 100,000 civilian casualties. Karim could still feel his father's strong arms, lifting him up to see the stars and laughing at some silly joke he had played. Whenever he was there, laughter and fun happened but Karim had taken a long time to be able to remember his dad as he was. Now that he was an adult, he felt the unfairness of it all, the years of pleasure having his Dad around would have given him especially now he had his own children.

When they arrived in Spain, his mother claimed asylum, they had no possessions with them, and had faced a lot of prejudice. Even now, some people still called them 'Arabs' which they used as a pejorative term for everyone originating from the Middle East. The little family had lived in the refugee camp for a year and Karim and his sister, Amina missed all their schooling other than the lessons that their mother made them learn. Finally, they had settled in Malaga and Karim and his sister had started school. Amina was two years younger than Karim and they had both studied hard. Their mother had worked at any job she could find to bring in money and had become a Spanish citizen. Karim and Amina had helped where they could by doing odd jobs for the neighbours, washing cars and carrying shopping. It had been a hard upbringing but both he and Amina were settled now in good jobs. Amina worked as a civil lawyer for a local firm, and he had become a police officer after finishing university, he felt he wanted to help people get justice for the crimes against them, a thing he would never be able to do for his father. He had his police job, his wife, Kyra, and his children. Between his sister and himself, they were able to look after their mother and make sure she wanted for nothing.

Karim was tall, he wore his dark hair long and he had developed the habit of pushing it back off his forehead every few minutes. He had large deep brown eyes, a long aquiline nose and a wide and generous mouth. Women always noticed him, but he seemed blissfully unaware of the effect he had on them, and each night went home to his wife and two children. He did his best to keep his family close and did not like his wife to work. After his experiences in Iran, he could not stand the thought of them being in danger. It had caused arguments of course but Kyra understood why he had that attitude; she filled her time with other things when he was at work and the children were at school. She didn't always tell him where she went as she knew it would cause and argument. Far better that he didn't know she had a part time job as an administrative assistant to a professor at the university, she was an intelligent woman and wouldn't be content just bringing up children which while it was a worthwhile job, she felt was not the be all and end all of existence.

Chapter 4

Armando was pleased to see that Elena Ruiz had arrived and had already started her work. He walked over to speak to her.

Jorge Moreno, her assistant, was busy recording, photographing and measuring the scene. A small tent had been erected over the body to keep away prying eyes and to keep the heat of the sun away. Armando looked at the body of the young woman and was saddened by her youth. It made him angry to think about a life cut short in such a senseless way.

"I think she may have fallen from one of the balconies above. You may find more evidence there, she has a nasty bruise on the side of her head, and I can see the impact bruising consistent with a fall from height, the blood spatter indicates she may have been alive when she fell." Elena Ruiz stood from her squatting position by the victim speaking as if they were already halfway through a conversation. She always got straight down to the business at hand. She knew the police would be under pressure to get results and so didn't waste time with greetings or small talk.

"You can see here the blood spatter on the side of the dumpster." She was in her usual white jumpsuit, blue gloves and shoe covers. Armando had wanted to ask her out for a long time but was afraid. Elena always seemed so unreachable, he felt awkward around her and so had not acted upon his feelings.

Snapping himself out of his reverie Armando returned his mind to the business at hand.

"So" he said weakly, looking at his watch as an excuse to take his eyes from hers. "Any chance of the time of death?"

"Well, I won't know for sure until I get her back to the lab but based on my initial temperature readings and the state of the body, I would say she died no more than 11 hours ago."

"So, in the early hours of this morning." Armando said.

"Yes, but I will confirm it in my report as soon as I can Detective"

"OK, thanks Elena. Let me know when you have more information. I need to know if she fell. Was it an accident or something worse? She is young but so many people suffer with their mental health these days anything is possible. Was there any identification on the body?"

"I haven't found any yet, so that will be your job, Armando. I'll know more about the cause of death when I return to my laboratory. I did find this…" she pointed to the leg of Iberico Ham on the floor. "I'm not sure why it is here; it is very odd. It could have fallen from the bin, or someone may have dropped it, however it is out of place and an expensive thing to lose so I will take it back to the lab."

Armando took a photo of the dead woman's face and also a detailed description of her hair, eye colour and her height, build and the clothes she was wearing. Then he left the forensic team to get on with their job while he tried to establish her identity. Officer Dominguez had told him he didn't think she was a local woman. As he knew most of the local population, Armando trusted his knowledge.

Elena watched Officer Ramirez walk to his car. He was in decent shape, he always looked smart, and she had often thought about asking him to go out to dinner with her but had been afraid it would ruin their professional relationship. Maybe she would ask him once this case was closed.

"Jorge, when we finish up here make sure everything is brought back to the lab, last time we attended an incident you left the samples on the pavement." barked Elena

Across from the alley a heavily built man in a leather jacket watched Elena and Jorge as they carried out their investigation. He hung back in the doorway of a closed shop, pretending to read a newspaper and playing with his phone. Too late to retrieve the ham, he needed to know what happened to it so he could get it later. His boss would give him hell for losing it. He didn't want to come across those two who worked for him, the last time he had seen those thugs they had made him feel as if they would prefer it if he stopped breathing.

Chapter 5

Armando walked around the corner to the letting agency in the Calle Rodrigo Acosta. He could have delegated this job but always preferred to be in the heart of the investigation. He knew the owner, Gabriella, they had been friends for many years.

The letting office was bright and airy with modern desks and chairs and Armando greeted Louisa, the petite receptionist, as he came up the steps and through the door.

Gabriella suddenly appeared from the back office, a vision in a floral top with a low neckline and a dogtooth patterned skirt.

"Armando" she shouted, looking up from under her eyelashes, "Where have you been? Too busy to visit a poor Spanish girl?"

"Hi Gabriella, Yes, a policeman's life is full of broken appointments, I'm sorry. This is not a social call either I'm afraid, I must ask you some questions."

"Is it about the young woman found this morning? What happened?" Gabriella adjusted her floral rimmed glasses and fixed Armando with a steely stare.

"How did you hear about it?" Was it the cleaner?" He asked

"Yes, poor Sofia. She was very shaken. Her husband came in with the laundry and keys for her and I said she could take tomorrow off."

"Can you give me a list of the apartments Sofia was working in this morning? Also, I wondered if you could identify the victim and let me know if she had rented an apartment from you? I have a picture of her, but I warn you it is from the scene, so not very nice." Armando showed the picture he had taken of the young woman. Gabriella looked at the photo and paled beneath her make up.

"Oh my God, the poor girl. Yes, I remember her, she is Ms Maisie Bright, she rented apartment D3 in the Plaza de Olvida for one month. Oh, what a shame, she seemed like a genuinely nice young woman and had lovely manners, she said she was here for a long rest."

"Is that all? Didn't she say why she needed to rest?"

"No, I presumed it was a broken heart…"

"You are required to photocopy the passport of anyone renting apartments from you Gabriella, did you?"

"Well of course Armando, do you think I would break the law? I would only do that if you promised to arrest me!" Armando smiled and shook his head as Gabriella went into the inner office and came back with a photocopy of the passport, the rental agreement and a list of Sofia's cleaning jobs for the day.

"You will also want the key to the apartment Armando. Here it is. Drop it back when you have finished."

"I will need forensics to sweep the place, so I hope you have not let the apartment again for a while."

He rang Elena and told her the apartment number.

"OK thanks Armando, I will come over when we have finished here."

Armando examined the passport photo and the rental agreement in more detail. He could see that in life Maisie Bright looked quite different. He looked at her place of birth: Ipswich, England. He would ring his boss, Martin

Jerez, after he had been to the apartment and tell him what he had discovered so far.

Saying his goodbyes to Gabriella, Armando left the letting agency and went straight to apartment D3 in the Plaza de Olvida Apartments, where he found that Sofia Verano Ortiz was an incredibly good cleaner, the apartment was spotless.

"She has probably eliminated some evidence." thought Armando with a sigh as he put on his nitrile gloves and shoe covers at the door of the apartment. On entering the apartment, he saw a small suitcase on the bed with its contents haphazardly replaced, he gave these a cursory look and saw the woman's passport, he checked the details with those that Gabriella had given him and bagged it up. He also found a leather wallet containing a warrant card from the Suffolk Police Force. Armando read the card. So, the woman was a police officer. He would have to add this information to the report to his boss and also to the British Police.

He wondered what the young woman had been doing. Was she really just on holiday or could she have been working undercover, if the latter were the case, should his department have been informed?

Armando was puzzled and looked again at the contents of the suitcase when a framed picture of a woman and a child caught his eye, the photo in the frame was a little crooked. Armando turned the frame over and examined the back and saw that a small edge of white paper was sticking out, he removed the back of the frame and the cardboard insert. He found the paper contained a list of dates of shipments from the Cabanillos Ham factory in Malaga. The next date was underlined in red. Armando reached into his pocket and pulled out an evidence bag, placing the list carefully inside. He also bagged the warrant card. . He stepped out onto the small balcony and looked over. It was directly above the place where Elena was examining the body. He was just about to go when he noticed a few small spots of something on the balcony railing, "it could be blood." he thought

Locking the apartment behind him and placing some police tape across the door Armando rang Elena again and told her what he thought he had found on the balcony of the apartment then he knocked on the door of apartment D4.

A sleepy man in a vest and boxer shorts opened the door. Scratching his undercarriage and his head simultaneously, while Armando asked if he had heard or noticed anything unusual from the apartment next door.

"No mate, I just woke up, didn't I? Heavy night wiv me mates, weren't it?" the man growled.

Armando blessed the fact that when he had been learning English, he had watched a British show called EastEnders, or he wouldn't have understood one word.

"What time did you return to the apartment?"

"I dunno do I, after 2am at least, is that all?" the man yawned and scratched some hidden itch.

"For now, yes, thank you Mr…"

"Fredricks, Bernie to you."

If you think of anything else Mr Fredricks, you can call me on this number," Armando handed the man his card.

Heading back to headquarters Armando spoke to his boss Chief Inspector Martin Jerez giving him an update on the little that he knew so far.

"I will call the British Consulate and you can do the rest. You can contact the police force and see what she was up to. I don't want any come back with this case so make sure you are thorough. I can't afford to have the mayor or anyone else breathing down my neck!" As usual Jerez sounded grumpy. Armando took no notice; he had learned that was Jerez's way. On the drive back to Malaga, questions ran round in Armando's head.

A girl had died. Maisie Bright, what was the cause of death? She was a police officer, why had she been in Nerja? Was it purely to take a holiday as she had told Gabriella? Why did she have a shipment list from Cabanillos packing plant?

Armando approached police headquarters and pulled into his usual parking space; he hoped that once he and Karim put their heads together, they would unravel some of the mystery surrounding Maisie Bright's death.

Armando had worked with Karim El Baz for the last 5 years; they knew each other's habits. Karim was not afraid to be honest if he thought Armando was wrong about something and Armando had relied on his good sense. Karim had been with him many times, providing back up when things got dangerous and saving Armando's life on more than one occasion.

Chapter 6

Armando logged onto his computer in the office and searched British police force details for Suffolk. He quickly found a phone number for their headquarters in Ipswich and dialled the long international number. After being transferred to five different people the phone was answered by a man with a deep voice.

"Inspector Last speaking. How can I help?"

His tone was almost bored, and Armando wondered if the Inspector really did want to help. Then he realised that the Inspector was probably under the same pressure as police officers everywhere. Crime was something that never took a day off.

"Hello, Inspector Last, my name is Officer Armando Ramirez of the Policia Nacional of Spain, I'm ringing you from Malaga, and I'm sorry to say I have some unwelcome news. Do you know a police officer called Melissa Bright, ID. number 568713?"

"I'm sorry Officer erm Ramirez did you say? Officer Ramirez, as you know we can't give details of our police officers over the phone. Can you tell me what this is about?"

Armando sighed; he couldn't see his boss paying for a flight to the UK. He decided to give his news to the Inspector, so he followed with...

"We've found a body. The woman that died, I believe, is one of your officers. I have her warrant card. Her name is Melissa Bright. ID 568713. I believe she worked for the Suffolk Constabulary."

Armando could hear the shocked silence at the other end of the phone line. He heard a chair being pushed away from a desk and a rush of breath followed by,

"Melissa, you say, my officer is always called Maisie for short. Yes, we do have an officer by that name. Did you say dead? I don't understand, she was on extended leave, can you tell me what happened?" Armando could imagine the shocked features of Inspector Last, he had lost a colleague in bad circumstances too and it was something that he would never forget.

"Inspector Last, I need someone to identify the woman formally and speak to any relatives. Are you able to arrange that? Do you know her parents? The British Consulate will be in touch with them, but it may help them to have somebody local to talk to."

"Yes, Officer Ramirez, there is only her mother I believe. I will ensure I speak to her."

"Thank you Inspector Last, I will send you a photograph of the victim so you can be sure we are talking about the same person."

"I don't want her mother reading about it in the newspaper. I have a few things to sort out, but I will try and be on the next available flight as soon as I have spoken to my boss and the family."

"Thank you, Inspector Last, sorry it is not better news. I will give you my personal number, please ring me when you have arranged your flight, I will meet you at the airport in Malaga." Armando ended the call and sat back in his chair. It was always the same at the start of a case, families to be informed, bodies to be identified and then the real work would begin.

He was hungry, it had been hours since he started work. He checked on Karim and saw that the incident room was well on its way to being organised.

"Karim, its lunchtime, shall we grab a quick bite before the forensics start coming in?"

"Yes boss, you read my mind."

They walked to the small tapas bar across the road, it was plain with wooden tables a good range of tapas and a sign on the wall that said,

"We don't have the internet so you will just have to talk to each other!"

Armando and Karim talked football and handball and the latest news from Spain and Karim's family. They didn't talk about the latest case they had as they both knew it may be their last opportunity to take a peaceful break before the real work started.

Chapter 7

On a farm near Haverhill in Suffolk, the spotted rare breed pigs in the field snuffled and rooted up the earth around their straw filled Nissan hut homes. It was raining and Joe Odreck had just plugged up the umpteenth hole in the roof of his farmhouse and was thoroughly fed up with the weather. He was sick of having no money for repairs and tired of the daily struggle to keep the farm afloat.

"Afloat" he mumbled to himself, "I'll need a bloody ark soon!"

However, he did love his pigs and they loved the mud. Joe was 40. He had wanted to be married by this age, but he had yet to find the right man. He was naturally shy, when he finally plucked up the courage to tell his mum he preferred men, he was amazed and touched when she said,
"I know that Joe, I just waited until you felt you could tell me in your own time. Everyone has the right to be loved. Just be yourself, Joe. You can't control what others think so let them get on with it. Be true to yourself."

Joe had been alone since his mother's death in the previous year, he missed her terribly and hadn't minded caring for her one bit. With the help of local nurses and carers he looked after her at home to the last. The time they had spent together in those last few months was exhausting and rewarding, just sitting by her holding her hand had been a pleasure and she died knowing that she was loved and had urged Joe to find someone special for himself.

Joe had been frightened by the prospect of going to a night club to meet other people. He found that living in the country, where wild boar roamed the forest, there were few other opportunities to meet that special someone. He had gone to the young farmers club once or twice but found it all a bit too laddish for him. So, he lived alone and was lonely and filled up his time with the farm. Thank goodness he had his pigs to look after.

Joe had never known his father, his Mum just said that the man she was supposed to marry was no good. Joe knew she had lived in Spain with her grandparents because her own parents had died when she was young. She didn't talk much about her early life, only that her mother, Joe's grandmother, had married a Spanish man she had met in Bury St Edmunds and that they had lived there until they had been killed in a car crash in 1961. Hence, Joe's Mum had been sent to live in Spain with her grandparents.

Joe's Great grandparents owned a pig farm too and raised pigs for Iberico ham. Joe had tried to ask about his father a few times over the years, he thought he had heard the name Cabano, but his mum just said he was best forgotten and refused to give him any further details.

Joe hadn't wanted to upset her, so he left it alone.

His mum, Maria, had been a housekeeper for an old Suffolk Farmer who left her the farm for taking good care of him as he had no other family.

Before she died his mother had told him that he would find some papers in the attic. She made him promise to find them. She had been a little confused during her last month's so Joe, unsure if she was imagining things or talking about something real, humoured her and said he would look for them. He wasn't sure if she had been in her right mind and after her death had not had the heart to go into the attic let alone search for the mysterious papers.

Joe knew he really should have cleaned out the attic by now but with everything else to look after on the farm he had put it to the bottom of his to do list.

"It'll wait," he thought. It had been a few months since he had last considered tackling the job. He knew he would have to clear the cavernous space in any case if he ever got the money together to fix the roof.

Joe leaned on the fence. He played with the hole that had just appeared in the sleeve of his old faithful brindled jumper. His deep brown hair protruded from beneath his flat cap as if it were trying to escape. He was about average height, wiry and muscular. He didn't need the gym, lifting all the bags of feed and hay bales kept him more than fit. His hazel eyes reflected the rolling Suffolk skies as he breathed in a good lungful of clean Suffolk air, even if it was tinged with odour of piggy, it was invigorating he thought. His green wellington booted foot rested on the bottom rail while he looked at his herd with pride. The Saddlebacks and Tamworths were perfectly happy rooting around in the mud. Sadie, the largest of the saddlebacks came and leaned on the fence. She was Joe's pet pig, he had hand reared her when her mum had rejected her. When she got too big for the house, he had moved her in with the herd and she immediately became the matriarch of the group. She had a white head and body with the black stripe across her shoulders giving the look of a saddle.

Saddlebacks were a very old breed of pig, a mix of Wessex and Essex pigs. They roamed wild in the New Forest and Joe had found out that in the wild they only lived for four or five years. Sadie was fifteen years old now, Joe knew she could live for twenty years or more. He scratched her back and she nuzzled his hand in a cat like manner. She had been a good mother to more than thirty piglets. Now she just lived with the herd, enjoying the outdoors. Smiling, Joe gave Sadie one final scratch and went to make another cup of tea.

Chapter 8

Senoras Gomez and Molinera sat in the shade of the umbrella on the balcony of the Café Ani, sipping their afternoon coffee and enjoying a sweet biscuit. They had conducted this ritual for many years. The café had a small balcony that jutted out over the beach giving a view of the azure sea beyond and the coastline as it curved towards Maro.

Senora Marguerite Gomez sat languidly in the café chair with her long legs crossed at the ankles. She was tall with a girlish figure barely changed from her teenage years; her clothes stylish yet understated. Today she wore a long line turquoise skirt and a plain cream blouse with a beautiful turquoise brooch pinned at the neck. She had many admirers in Nerja but never committed to anyone, she had only begun to live properly after getting away from her brutal husband. Despite the fact he had abused and beaten her she had regained some confidence and was determined to live a full life. If a man asked her to dinner, she would accept and after an enjoyable evening, leave them to go home alone. She never invited them back to her house.

She refused to live in a prison of her bad experiences with Rafael, but she could not bring herself to take her relationships any further. She kept Senora Molinera amused with descriptions of her confused suitors.

Senora Berta Molinera marvelled at Marguerite's complicated lifestyle, enjoying these tales of the unexpected. Of course, she knew about Marguerite's tragic marriage, Marguerite had confided in her long ago, in an afternoon of Spanish rain and tears.

Berta was glad that her own life had been more tranquil and her marriage to Jose had been happy until his employer had told her he had been killed in a "tragic accident falling into the machinery." Berta was not so sure it had been an accident. The machine in the ham factory where he was a night security guard had many safety features, most of the machinery was not open and had lids on any hoppers to stop anything or anyone falling in. All the machinery should have been switched off as Jose made his rounds, he knew how dangerous it was and wouldn't have gone anywhere near it if the motors had been running. The night he had died they said that some engineers had been working on the machinery earlier that day and that he had simply fallen into it. Of course, the management denied any wrongdoing. The override switch was on which meant the blades in the machines could have been exposed. They said that after falling into the machinery parts of his poor body had been chopped and packaged efficiently in twenty minutes, long before the day staff arrived and made their terrible discovery. Management had blamed Jose. They said he was drunk. No one had really investigated properly; she had even heard people joking that he would have to be buried before his sell by date! It was very hurtful, and Berta shuddered to think of it even now.

The tragedy had left her in reduced circumstances because they said Jose was at fault. She did not receive his pension and she had had to rely on the wage she earned at the office at the Sierra High School, where she worked as an administration assistant, and their meagre savings to make ends meet. The recession in Spain had not helped her any and she was glad that she and Jose were able to buy the small house in the Plaza de Olvida and pay for it fully before he died. Today's events had forced the memory of Jose's death back into her mind with a jolt. She was feeling very nervous, her cup rattled in the saucer as she replaced it after taking a sip of her afternoon coffee.

Berta had a soft figure that children loved to snuggle against. She was shorter than Marguerite and they looked an odd pair as they walked anywhere together.

"That police officer was handsome, didn't you think Berta?" Marguerite smiled as she asked the question, she wanted to distract Berta from thoughts of her husband's death and also, she knew that Berta only ever had eyes for her Jose and was always scandalised that she commented on handsome young men.

"Marguerite, that officer was less than half your age, honestly!" Berta laughed

"I'm not dead Berta, I can still look, can't I?" Said Marguerite laughing

"I know you Marguerite and you enjoy looking a bit too much."

Marguerite smiled and thought of the young police officer and took another sip of her excellent coffee.

She had rid herself of her violent husband and escaped with her life. She had run from Madrid to Nerja, told everyone she was a widow, reverted to her maiden name and had lived happily alone for more than 30 years, first over the dress shop in town and now in her small house on the Carabao.

The Carabeo was a winding street that led from the town centre to the beaches in the west of the town. It was quiet and held a mix of small traditional Spanish houses and larger properties with sea views from the gardens. Bougainvillea trailed down from balconies and palm trees swayed above the beaches. Marguerite's house was on the sea facing side of the street and she loved to sit each morning on her balcony, take in the salt filled air, marvelling anew at the ever-changing colours of the Mediterranean. She would watch the wild cats and kittens that lived on the beach below, chasing each other and stalking the mice that lived in the undergrowth, shaded by the vegetation sprouting from the crevices in the rocky walls above the beach. Each day the cats waited for Juan, an old fisherman, who trudged down the uneven steps to the beach from the Carabao. Dressed in baggy jeans and a checked shirt with an old red anorak, his faced etched by his years living and working by the sea, Juan brought the cats their lunch of fish heads and other waste pieces, waiting for them to make an appearance he emptied the bags of food on which they gorged themselves eagerly. Once full they disappeared back to the undergrowth or just lay contented in the sun basking in the heat of the day. Marguerite now had enough money to lead a comfortable life. She had almost stopped worrying daily about her husband Rafael although sometimes a picture of him came to her in her sleep and she would wake up trembling.

Chapter 9

Joe's mum, Maria, had arrived at the farm to live with her grandparents, Her grief at her parents death was still very painful, her grandmother provided plenty of warmth and affection and held her in the night when she woke crying, she could speak little Spanish, her father had taught her, but it never seemed to matter too much to her grandmother who was able to convey love and affection without the need for words. Sometimes she sang to Maria to get her to sleep. Maria found it hard at first to keep up with the speed of conversation between her grandparents, but she soon learned.

They worked hard tending the pigs and making sure they were fit and healthy. There was plenty of food for the pigs and for the humans. Maria grew up, her cheeks freckled in the sun and her arms and legs tanned. Maria loved the farm and though the work was hard she was able to cope with the many chores each day. Her grandparents also made sure she went to school and did her homework, they wanted her to go to university, she was bright and outgoing and loved to paint and draw. The farmhouse was littered with her pictures tacked to the walls. Her grandmother, Inez, loved them and would never throw any of them away.

The summer before Maria was due to go to college her grandfather decided to take on some help, after all he was getting older and couldn't manage some of the heavier jobs on the farm. He had taken on a local lad from the orphanage. He was 17 and was able to carry out all the tasks Maria's granddad needed done. Maria had taken an instant dislike to him, He was good looking enough but his eyes were icy. He seemed to always be watching her with a smirk on his lips. Maria had tried to avoid him whenever she could. She was relieved when he went back to the orphanage at the end of the summer.

Her university course in fine arts was due to start at Easter and she was looking forward to living in Malaga. She was ready for the adventure but knew she would miss her grandparents terribly. Still, she would be home for the holidays. Her course was in the El Ejido campus, and she would live in a room with a family nearby. Soon she was in a whirlwind of study, meeting new people and enjoying the course.

One night when she was returning to her lodgings, she caught sight of a boy she thought she knew. It was getting dark so she couldn't see his face properly but something about him was familiar.

Maria thought no more of it, but the following week she received some flowers, just a small bunch of wildflowers. There was a card with her name but no other message. It had been left on her doorstep.

Maria thought it must be one of the other students playing games with her.

A couple of months later, before the start of the summer break she found a note on her desk in the studio where she and the other students worked.

"Have a good holiday, mi amora" it had scrawled on it.

Maria screwed it up and threw it in the bin. She had no time for silly games. If a boy liked her, he was free to ask her out!

Summer break came and Maria took the long bus ride home to the farm of her grandparents.

Grandmother Inez had laid on a feast. Her grandfather Jose was hovering around until he could give her a big hug.

"Well, how is my next Sorolla? Will you soon be famous nieta?"

"No Grandfather, I don't think I am that good."

"Rafael is here again this summer to help."

Maria stiffened as Rafael strutted in and took his place at the table.

"Welcome home Maria" he said, "Hopefully we will spend some time together this summer." He leered across at her.

"I will be very busy, I'm sorry, I have a lot of work to do for college over the summer." She coldly snapped.

A look crossed Rafael's face that made Maria shudder. She resolved to keep out of his way as much as she could.

Just before the end of the holidays, Maria had been painting in the forest, the sun had been just at the right angle and shone through the trees in columns. A gentle breeze rustled the leaves, and the birds were singing as if the song would be their last.

Maria leaned back and took in the scene, she would miss the tranquillity of it all when she went back to university.

A twig snapped behind her and she felt a knife at her throat.

"Well, Maria, I have you to myself at last." A flat voice said. "Now remove those clothes, if you please."

Maria pushed back and tried to run but he was too strong for her.

"Rafael, what are you doing?"

"What I should have done ages ago you stuck up bitch, teach you a lesson. Now clothes!"

Maria began to remove her dungarees, then her shirt. Rafael stepped forward and ripped it open then taking the knife he cut her bra.

"That's better. Now turn around."

Again, Maria tried to run but Rafael was on her, he knocked her to the ground, holding her with one hand while he ripped her underwear and loosened his trousers.

"Now you will know what a real man is like, not those pretty boys at university. Yes, I have seen them prancing about with their long hair."

"No Rafael, please don't. "Maria began to cry.

"That's it princess, beg!" he pushed himself inside her and laughed when he found she was still a virgin.

The attack seemed to go on for hours to Maria, he bit and punched her, slapping her when she cried out and bruising her wrists by holding them above her head.

When he had finished, he took the knife and trailed it down her body.

"You are mine now. Maria. Don't forget and don't go running telling tales to your grandparents or I will kill them and make you watch. Say "Yes Rafael"

"Yes." She stuttered.

"Remember I am watching you, I know where you stay in Malaga and at the University."

Maria trembled

"I will visit you whenever I want." He laughed. "Say Yes Rafael."

"Yes Rafael." She said through her tears.

"Now go! Remember what I said."

With that he was gone. Maria laid on the grass looking up at the sky, the scene now ruined for her forever. She dressed as well as she could and ran back to the farm.

Her grandmother noticed her dishevelled appearance as soon as she came home,

"What happened Maria?" she asked

"I fell Abuela, I ripped my clothes that's all." Maria struggled to keep her voice steady. "I'm fine. I will go and bathe and be down in a while for dinner. Don't worry."

Maria's grandmother knew something wasn't right and when Rafael came in and she saw his self-satisfied face she felt that there was something more serious going on.

Maria bathed and tried to scrub away Rafael's touch. Eventually she dressed and went back to the kitchen. Rafael picked up his knife and began playing with it.

Maria said nothing, her nerves were in shreds, she had to try and keep her hands from shaking, she couldn't let her grandparents know and so she went back to university at the end of the week as planned.

Coming home to her lodgings the next week she again saw the figure across the street watching her, she was sure it was Rafael. She was sure he would never leave her alone, he thought he had a hold over her now, but he was wrong.

Maria had saved a little money and some of her friends were going to London for a short break before Christmas, she decided to tag along and try to stay there. She would get away from Rafael forever. She telephoned her grandparents and told them that she had been offered a place in England studying art and would be going immediately. She was sorry there was no time to visit and say goodbye, but she would write once she was settled.

Once in England she had moved to Suffolk and got a job as a housekeeper for an old farmer with no family. They got on well and Maria was used to farm work although the English winter was harder to take. By Christmas she knew she was pregnant. With trepidation she told the old farmer who smiled and said

"If I can't tell when a lady, cow or pig is pregnant by now dear I should have given up farming long ago. You and the kiddie can stay here. I could do with the company. Be nice to see a young 'un round the place."

Maria threw her arms round the old farmer's neck and kissed his stubbly cheek.

Chapter 10

Elena Ruiz worked long hours in the lab in Malaga. Elena had worked hard to become the chief forensic officer. She had fought against the machismo that was the norm for many Spanish males. It had been one of her greatest battles and she was pleased that she had managed to earn the respect of most of the die-hard sexists in the organisation. Her parents were both in professional careers, her mum was a doctor, and her father owned a tutoring company for special needs learners. They had been able to support her ambition to succeed and encouraged her to reach for the stars, whatever path she chose. Her father had bought her a small moped when she moved to Malaga along with a small apartment near her office. The moped had made it easy for her to navigate the narrow streets of Nerja and many of the other whitewashed towns in the region.

Once back in the lab Elena changed into a clean set of scrubs, hair net and gloves and turned her attention to the body of the young woman. Jorge had already prepared the body for examination by placing it on the mortuary table fully clothed in the pyjama shorts and t-shirt she was wearing when she had been killed. The identification number and tag had also been prepared and Elena was pleased to see all the equipment she would need was laid out neatly. The lab was not the most modern building, but it was well equipped with the latest instruments. Once undressed the tag would be tied to Maisie's big toe.

Elena started with Jorge assisting, by taking a good look at the young woman's body, front and back and photographing her.

After removing the clothes Elena again examined the body closely for any marks and again photographed her front and back. She photographed the bruising on her neck and the head injury, she also found bruises on her arms consistent with trying to fend off an attack and there was also a large bruise just below her ribs. After weighing and measuring, including the taking of an x-ray, she took fingerprints. It was a methodical and thorough business and Elena made sure all the steps were followed including examining the clothing for fibres or any remnant of the perpetrator. DNA swabs, bodily fluids, blood samples, hair and fibres on the woman's clothes.

Elena found tissue under her fingernails and removed it to be sent for DNA analysis. This would all assist the police in finding the killer. There was no evidence of any sexual motive for the young woman's death. A fall from height had been the cause, following a fight in which the woman had been partially strangled and thrown from the balcony. A fall of 11 to 15 ft was enough to cause a fatality. The injuries to her head, abdomen and pelvis and thorax all pointed to the conclusion of a fall from height. This was the cause of death. The victim had been partially strangled before being thrown from the balcony. The injuries to her arms showed defensive bruising and livid bruising round the neck, indicating that she had been throttled.

The time of death she estimated by taking the temperature of the corpse, however factors such as the heat of the day or night would make a difference. Elena thought it may have been between midnight and five in the morning. She documented and photographed all her findings; she would prepare her report and have it ready for Armando and also ring him to give him an update. Elena knew that he would be under pressure to close this case as quickly as possible.

"Thanks Jorge" Elena said "You can put her away for now, I know you have to leave for a dental appointment. I can deal with the rest."

After returning the young woman to the grey drawer in the cooler Jorge left for his appointment.

Elena retrieved the mysterious joint of ham found at the scene and began her examination. She photographed the label focusing on the maker's name and batch number. She took a swab of the wrapping to test for anything unusual, she carefully removed the net cover and placed it in an evidence bag. Elena selected a large knife from the instrument table to cut the wrapping when she found an incision had already been made in the thickest part of the joint under the label, and a pouch of plastic had been inserted inside it. It was such a neat job that Elena almost missed it. Elena stopped and inspected the cut; she carefully photographed the contents in situ and after she had removed the pouch from its hiding place, she saw that it contained some sort of powder. Taking a small drill, she pierced a hole in the plastic packing. She removed some of the powdery contents with a spatula and placed it into a small bag along with a cocaine reagent. She then shook the bag and the contents turned blue, a positive test for cocaine.

Once Elena had cleared away and documented the evidence from the ham, she returned to her desk and began to type up her conclusions, turning to pick up her phone to call Armando, she heard the door to the laboratory opening.

"Who's there?" she called out.

The lights in the corridor flickered and went out.

At first Elena thought that the caretaker had mistakenly put them out, not realising that she was still at work, she walked round the mortuary table to the door, opened it and looked out into the dark corridor. A blow caught her on the back of the head, she fell, motionless to the floor. The large, hooded figure stepped over her and entered the lab.

Chapter 11

Armando had just started to fall asleep when the telephone started ringing. The phone rang and rang until at last Armando realised through his semi dreamlike fog that he needed to answer it. The time on his phone told him it was barely midnight.

"Si, it's Officer Ramirez. Who is this?"

"It is officer Alvarez sir, I know that Elena Ruiz, the forensic officer, is a friend of yours. She has been found at her office, by the caretaker. It looks as if someone may have attacked her. She is unconscious and has been brought to the hospital. I was called to the scene, and I thought you should know. I know you are close friends. I have rung her parents, but they live in Cordoba and will take a while to get here."

"Thanks Alvarez, stay there. I'm on my way." Armando wondered if he and Elena were being talked about at the station, cops were such gossips it wouldn't surprise him. Something about the way Alvaraz had said "Good Friends" had triggered his curiosity.

He got up quickly, dressed in the first thing that came to hand. Then grabbing his jacket, he hurried down to his car. As he drove to the hospital, he began to think about what happened to Elena, his stomach turned at the thought of her being hurt. It struck him at that moment how much he cared for her and he scolded himself for not making his feelings known.

Armando flashed his ID at the receptionist and enquired where Elena was being treated. She directed him to the third-floor, room twelve. Running up the stairs of the four-storey building Armando smelt the antiseptic aroma of the hospital wards, he heard the muted sounds of the nursing staff exchanging information and turned right. Along the corridor a doctor was just leaving room 12, Armando approached him and tapped him on the arm introducing himself and asking.

" How is she, doctor?"

"Well, she's had a fairly substantial blow to the head and is very groggy, the C.T. scan showed nothing significant, we'll keep her here overnight for observation, but I'm confident she'll recover, and she can probably go home tomorrow if all is well."

"Thank you, doctor, may I go and see her?" The relief showed clearly on Armando's face.

"Yes, but not too long. She needs to rest."

The sight of Elena, lying in the hospital bed with a bandage covering the deep gash on the left side just below the hairline made Armando see red. Who could have done this? He'd soon get the bastards.

Armando approached Elena's bedside and took her hand,

"Elena, it's me, Armando. Can you hear me?"

"Can't you see when a girl is trying to sleep?" she said sleepily." Coming in here all doe eyed, of course I can hear you, I'm not deaf." Elena smiled, her face was pale under her freckles, she looked very frail. Armando had never seen her looking so vulnerable.

"Thank God, Elena. What happened? Can you remember anything? Are you feeling up to answering some questions?"

"Yes, if you don't count the pain in my head. I can't tell you much. I heard a noise, then the lights went out and so did I."

"You were working very late, was the caretaker around?"

"It was about 9pm, so not that late and he usually does his rounds two or three times in the evening." Elena rubbed her head and her eyes closed momentarily, "They said he was the one who found me, but I don't know anything else." Elena yawned, struggling to keep her eyes open.
"I wonder why you were attacked; do you think it was a burglary?"

"I had just started to look at the ham joint we found at the scene. It contained a pouch of cocaine hidden in the meat. It was a very neat job, I nearly missed it. I was just about to ring you when I heard a noise, and the corridor lights went out and I woke up here. That's all I remember. " She rubbed her eyes.

"We now know that the dead girl was a police officer from England. I have spoken to them, and her boss is coming over here. Hopefully, we will know more soon. You must rest Elena; I have put a police officer at the door. You may still be in danger, and I'm not taking any chances. I'll come back tomorrow."

Elena was already asleep by the time he left the room. Armando had a quick word with Alvarez telling him to remain stationed at the door of Elena's room and he would send someone to relieve him.

When Armando left the hospital, he went home to shower and change and then returned to police headquarters. Karim had sent him a message earlier to say that he was off home.

Armando wanted to gather his thoughts and go over what had been discovered so far. He was too wound up to sleep anymore and thought he might as well do some work while it was quiet so that he could direct the investigation with a clear plan in mind.

When morning arrived, he found he had fallen asleep at his desk. He sat up and rubbed his stiff neck. He stood, his limbs rigid from the chair and stamped his feet. He poured himself a muddy cup of coffee from the pot and drank it down in one, pulling a face at the bitterness of over-stewed caffeine then headed straight out to Elena's laboratory. He arrived to see that Jorge was just going through the main door and talking animatedly to the caretaker.

"Oh! I just found out about Elena. If only I had been here, she would be OK." Jorge fidgeted back and forth on the balls of his feet. "If only I hadn't left early!"

"Yes, it is quite a shock. The doctor said she will recover after some rest. I need your help now Jorge, let us go in and you can tell me everything? Elena said that the ham she bought back had contained hidden drugs. I will need to see it?"

Armando guided Jorge by the elbow towards the laboratory. They both donned gloves before entering, and Armando asked Jorge to call a colleague to sweep the area for fingerprints or any other evidence of an assailant.

"It must be in the cold store. Wait here please." Jorge disappeared into the back of the lab. Armando waited for what seemed a very long time before Jorge reappeared.

"I'm sorry inspector the meat is not there."

"I'm not sure what has happened to it." "There is this…" Jorge held up the cocaine test. "It was lying under the shelf. Elena was preparing to take a closer look at the ham as I left."

Armando thought the only explanation could be that Elena's assailant had taken the ham. He saw the camera used for recording evidence and asked Jorge to show him the photos Elena said she had taken, but that was blank. There was no record of her examination of the ham nor, barring the test package, of anything else. All that remained was the voice recording Elena had made as she worked as this was stored on the lab's central system, not just on Elena's computer.

"Don't touch anything else Jorge. Once the lab has been swept for evidence we will continue"

Jorge nodded and said he would ask an assistant from another lab to come and help him. He also had plenty of paperwork to do once that was done.

"Thank you, Jorge, I'll need to take a copy of the voice recording back to the station, can you do that for me?

Jorge accessed the computer system and transferred a copy of Elena's voice recording onto a flash drive and gave it to Armando.

Armando asked at the reception desk if there was CCTV, and the security guard took him to the room with the CCTV monitors. In the darkened room he ran the tapes of the corridor and lab that covered the previous evening, A large figure wearing a dark hooded top was seen entering the corridor and switching off the lights, after that Armando could only see shadows, he asked if any cameras covered the outside of the building and after bagging them for evidence, he took these tapes with him too. It was enough to catch the man's exit carrying something heavy. He would see if the technical team at the station could enhance the quality of the tapes so that he could get a better picture of the man and allow him to be identified. He would also see if any of the cameras on the outside of the building had picked up the man entering or leaving.

He returned to the station and asked Karim to review all the CCTV footage and take an officer to see if any of the buildings in the vicinity of the lab had CCTV of the area.

"Ok. We'll meet here later and go over the evidence and plan what to do next. The detective from Suffolk should be here tomorrow so his input may also be useful."

Chapter 12

When Marguerite returned home after her afternoon coffee with her friend Berta, a small package had been left outside her door. Looking up and down the street and seeing no one she took the package indoors to open it. Inside was a crystal decanter top, wrapped in blood red tissue paper. Her hand shook as she remembered the last time she had seen it on that terrible night when she had run for her life. She saw it in her mind's eye, skittering across the marble floor and stopping at Rafael's feet, giving him the excuse to brutalise her. She shoved it back into the package and threw the whole thing into the bin. Though visibly shaken she refused to give in to the fear that was now invading her peaceful existence.

Chapter 13

Armando had been a police officer for fifteen years and had worked his way steadily up the ranks. His parents had been disappointed in his career choice. They hoped he would become an accountant like his father or a lawyer. Something respectable. Instead of that he would be mixing with criminals and seeing the worst of people all his life.

To Armando, the thought of sitting behind a desk all week and dealing with grey corporate people left him cold. When his best friend Hector, was killed in a random knife attack and died in his arms Armando made his mind up to join the police and put criminals away behind bars. Hector, had been twenty years old, the only child of elderly parents. Armando had grown increasingly angry as he watched them deal with the pointless loss of their only son and with the inability of the police to catch the killer. Hector's killer had never been caught and Armando had vowed to keep searching for him. He kept a file about the murder in the spare room at his apartment and hoped that something new would come to light that might allow him to bring the killer to justice.

His memory of that terrible night had not faded. He could still hear the rasping breath of his friend and feel the fading pulse in his neck. Armando had put pressure on the wound and held his friend, talking to him. The pavement had been washed and he could still feel the damp coming through the knee of his trousers. He could smell the iron tang of blood, pouring out of Hectors body. The ambulance seemed to take an age to get to them and Armando had watched as the light flickered in his friends' eyes and then went out. Armando had started CPR and the ambulance crew arrived to find him still trying to revive his friend, they had taken over and put Hector into the ambulance still trying to revive him, but their faces told Armando it was useless. They had been friends since the first day of school and had spent most of their school and college years together, chatting up girls, playing handball and enjoying many nights out. Armando still missed those times with his friend, he would never forget him.

Chapter 14

Two weeks before Maisie Bright's body was found, she had arrived in Nerja to embark upon her mission to find out more about the origin of the drugs that had ended up in Suffolk. She had tried to get information from the drug team at the station but with little success. She had even tried to transfer to that department but had been unsuccessful. Inspector Last had told her she wasn't ready and to concentrate on gaining some experience in his team before transferring. He would be more than happy to support her in 12 months or so. It was only when she saw the name Cabanillos on a document that had been left in the photocopier, regarding suspicious drugs activity between Malaga and Ipswich that she had decided to do some of her own digging. While drug crime was on the increase in Suffolk with Bury St Edmunds and Ipswich being the most affected the rest of the county was fairly safe. Maisie had done some research at home on the Cabanillos factory and had decided to travel to Spain and do some investigations of her own. She felt she owed it to her brother to punish the dealers and suppliers.

There had been a particularly nasty incident at work in which Maisie had been assaulted by a suspect on a raid, she had been trapped in one of the upstairs rooms of the house they raided by the suspect, who was hiding behind the door. It was her own fault, she had gone ahead of her colleagues, against procedure, she should have waited for her team as she entered the room, she made another mistake of not checking behind the door, the suspect had closed the door behind her, he had punched her several times and kicked her causing some very nasty bruised ribs, then grabbing her throat and trying to strangle her before her colleagues got there to drag him off.

Maisie was lucky her assailant had not had a weapon. Since her brother Stuart, had died from a drug overdose a year before she had been desperate to find the source of the drugs coming into Suffolk.

Her big brother had developed his drug habit at university, before that he was intelligent and caring and had always looked out for her when they were younger. That had all been wasted when drugs took hold of him and he became an addict and she saw a kind caring brother become manipulating and self-seeking, caring only about his next hit.

Maisie had watched her mum's heart break as she missed another piece of jewellery, or cash from her purse and couldn't put the loss down to her own carelessness.

Maisie had tried to help him, getting him a place in rehab twice, but he had always returned to drugs. His body had been discovered in the stairwell of the town centre car park. Her colleagues had supported her, but she had become obsessed, following the dealers on her days off, hoping to find the boss. She had told her superior, Inspector Last, nothing of this, but he had noticed the subtle changes in her behaviour and had warned her several times about sticking to procedure, along with advising her to get enough rest. So, when she had asked for a leave of absence due to stress, it had been granted and she took a month off work.

After Maisie had found all the information she could about the Cabanillos Jamon factory while in Suffolk. Her next step had been to travel to Malaga and arrange a visit with Mr Fernandez the Sales Manager of the Cabanillos factory in the city. She had made an appointment to see him before leaving the UK, saying she was starting a new delicatessen business and had heard his products were the best but before she ordered any she wondered if he would be able to take her on a tour.

Her visit to the factory had been easy, Senor Fernandez was very welcoming and hardly asked her any questions about her company, he was simply keen to impress a new customer. She arrived a little early for her appointment and tour. She wore a green dress covered with a smart jacket and matching shoes. She was five feet eight inches tall, short blond hair, green eyes and had a trim figure, she practiced yoga and loved running.

Running often helped her to clear her head and think things through when the stress of the job got too much, and she was then able to plan her next moves.

The sound of the leaves under her feet created a pleasant rhythm along with the aroma of early morning mist on the grass.

Maisie showed the security guard her letter and signed in. She could feel the stares of the factory workers as she walked past them. Senor Fernandez, a middle-aged greying man with a condescending smirk, was waiting for her, his hand held out he said,

"Miss Bright, delighted to meet you. Please follow me. We must don our food safety overalls as the glorious EU dictates."

Maisie knew she would have to wear a hat, overalls and shoe covers. Her hair was short, so the hat was no problem. She had also brought a pair of flat trainers to swop for her green shoes. She followed Senor Fernandez through a narrow doorway into a dimly lit corridor, up a flight of stairs and into a large office with several desks, computers glowing with the day's tasks. The same, unfortunately, couldn't be said for the staff who seemed to be positively glum. Maisie made a mental note of it all, she would transfer it to her notebook later. After a coffee, Senor Fernandez led the way down a different flight of stairs to a large changing room. They passed through the doorway to the area where they put on their protective clothing. Maisie swished through a plastic door onto the factory floor. The change in temperature made her shiver as she took in her surroundings. They were in a large loading bay with doors at one end. A lorry pulled up, its reverse warning signal bleeping as the workers stood by ready to unload and transport the meat to the first stage of making the medal winning Iberico Ham. At the far end of the loading bay another lorry was being unloaded. These crates were pushed through a door that looked like it led to a separate area of the factory. The men working in that area looked and acted differently to the other workers, their body language seemed to Maisie to be more aggressive, she tried to hang back to see what was happening, but Senor Fernandez took her by the elbow and swiftly guided her away from the area hurrying her onto the next part of the tour.

"As you can see Ms Bright, here at Cabanillos Ham we have a modern and partly automated process but be assured the traditions and quality of Iberico is still held in high regard. You can see the pork being delivered ready for our team of butchers to trim the excess fat and a large percentage of the skin so that the ham can breathe during curing. The legs are then layered in sea salt, this has antibacterial qualities, and they will stay in the salt containers for ten to fourteen days depending on weight. Come, we will see the next process."

As they walked through the curing area surrounded by the legs of pork hanging above her head, Maisie took it all in. She had researched the method of making Iberico Ham, but it was not this process that interested her, she wanted to find out how and when the drugs got to Suffolk and what part the factory played in the operation. She had very little time but needed to go to Senor Fernandez office and find evidence of the suppliers and the shipments of Ham. Maisie patiently followed Senor Fernandez around the factory, she saw that it was split into two sectors, one dealt with the whole legs of ham and the other was a packaging plant for the slices normally sold in supermarkets. It had a large conveyor belt that transported the meat for slicing and packaging with a walkway overhead that she assumed was for engineers to carry out maintenance. Each hopper for the meat had a lid so that nothing could fall in by mistake.

Once they were safely ensconced in Senor Fernandez's office Maisie began to ask her questions. "Thank you, Senor Fernandez, that was a remarkably interesting tour. I'm impressed by the cleanliness of your factory, but my clients are worried about suppliers who are not so scrupulous, I'm sure you would agree that my new venture wants only the best stock. The customers I will have will be very discerning. I cannot be too careful."

"Ahh, Miss Bright, sadly not everyone is as meticulous as we are. All our suppliers are carefully checked each year and we do not accept poor standards. No! This can never happen! We mainly use ham from our Andalusian farm here, it is near Cordoba in the Viajes Valle de Los Pedroches, on the edge of the Sierra de Hornachuelos National Park. We have a farm there that supplies us exclusively. The pigs are then taken to a local abattoir which we inspect at regular intervals to make sure they are doing everything correctly. You see Senorita Bright the pigs must be treated well at every stage or the meat will be tough. We also have other sites in this part of Spain as the farm near Cordoba could not supply all our needs. Be assured that all of our factories adhere to the strict standards we dictate." Senor Fernandez sat back in his chair with a smug look and crossed his arms over his portly belly.

"But, Senor Fernandez, surely in this day and age it is possible for less reputable suppliers to supply fake, poor-quality hams?" Maisie interjected; eyes wide.

"Miss Bright, we have the highest standards here. The pigs live on a diet of acorns, grass and herbs. They are raised free and happy, until their death of course, when they are transported here, as you witnessed this morning, for processing. We sell the whole legs and also more convenient packages for domestic use. As you can see from our pride wall, we have won many prizes." He raised his arm and pointed proudly to the certificates that lined the wall behind his desk. "Our reputation would be damaged if things were ever otherwise."

"When do the shipments go out and to where, Senor Fernandez? I would be interested to hear about the whole operation."

"We usually ship every month as the hams take time to cure and our customers are happy to wait for quality. I have a team at the loading bay, loading and unloading the lorries. We sometimes have shipments that must be sent out in the early hours of the morning and so we have a team for those times too.

"I saw some crates going to a different area from the others, what were they for?" Senor Fernandez looked up sharply and she thought he looked worried for a split second before he came back to his oily self.

"Just herbs and spices, nothing to worry about dear" He said. "As you can see Miss Bright, we have security here day and night and we take it very seriously!"

"I read that a security guard had been killed while working here at night." Maisie had received this bit of intelligence from newspapers she had read during her research. "What happened?" she asked innocently

"The man was stupid! He fell into a machine. He was drunk! His wife stirred up a lot of trouble, but you can't believe everything you read. It was a tragic accident caused by the man's carelessness, nothing more. He had overridden safety buttons no doubt by falling against them!"

Masie let the subject drop but hadn't believed one word of Senor Fernandez' explanation. She needed to know more about the night-time operation and the area of the loading bay she had not had access to. She planned to go back to the factory and observe the night watchman's routine before trying to find out any more information, she may have to go into the factory at night and search the offices.

Chapter 15

Officer Dominguez was less than pleased to be dragged along with Karim El Baz. He felt he was being used; it would only lead to Karim taking all the credit for anything that was found. He walked sulkily beside him.

"I really need your help, Dominguez, I know I'm taking liberties" Karim said. "Your knowledge of the locals is much better than mine and you have an easy way about you. I hope it will help us get some more witnesses or CCTV of the lab. You have worked in Malaga as well as Nerja, haven't you?"

Dominguez opened his mouth but was a bit stumped as to what to say. He was surprised that Karim knew about his time in Malaga. He was also surprised that he had been asked for help.

"Well, if you put it that way, I have to help you." Replied Dominguez, still a little put out.

"Yes, and if I'm late home again tonight, my wife will kill me! So, you may also be preventing murder!" Karim smiled

Dominguez wondered if he had been wrong about Karim El Baz, but still couldn't get over the idea that he was a foreigner.

As they walked Karim said

"Where do you live, Dominguez? Are you from Nerja?"

"Yes, I have lived here all my life, it is a wonderful place to live and bring up a family. My mother and father still live here too."

"You are lucky, Dominguez, my father was killed in the gulf war and my mother, sister and I had to leave Iran. When we came here, we had nothing, but the Spanish government took us in and most of the people we met were kind, so we were able to progress slowly. My mother worked hard at all sorts of low paid jobs to see us through school and as soon as my sister and I were old enough we were able to pitch in. We are grateful to Spain and were proud to make it our home after all we have been through. Iran will always be in our hearts, but we are safer here even today. Do you have children, Dominguez?"

"Yes, I have a wife and child, they are my world." Dominguez replied. "What about you?"

"I have two children. They are really Spanish. They often start a sentence in Arabic and finish in Spanish, they are hard enough to understand at the best of times without mixing the languages together. I try to teach them about Iran and their heritage. It is important to know where you come from, don't you think?"

Dominguez was thoroughly confused, he had never had a conversation with Karim, and it seemed that they shared a lot in common.

"My name's Pedro, why don't you call me Karim." Dominguez put out his hand and shook Karim firmly, resolving to look again at his attitude to foreigners. We all want the same thing, he thought, to be safe and for our families to thrive.

Chapter 16

Senor Rafael Cabanillos stood looking at the commercial district of Madrid, fifteen floors below him. He hated the city, these days he would rather be raising horses in Andalusia. The lifestyle and the people had all lost their shine. As he got older, he thought more and more about the life he had led, the things he had done to achieve his status, women he had known and who had left him, disappointments over the years at the lack of an heir to continue the business thanks to that stupid wife of his, Marguerite, she had failed to give him a son and was completely useless. Still, he had let her run, even though he knew exactly where she was. He didn't forget, he would get his revenge one day.

He was tired of wheeling and dealing, of younger caballeros who thought they knew it all, of the constant stress of staying at the top of the shark pond. He turned and observed his reflection in the mirror. He was of average height and in decent shape for a man of 68, his hair was greying at the edges and his smooth face was the result of the lightest touch from the surgeon's knife and regular visits to a very discreet beauty practitioner for Botox injections. His grey suit was made by the best tailors in Madrid. He smoothed down the front of his jacket. He had one more deal to do, and then he planned to retire to the country and live the life of a Spanish gentleman.

He had returned to the farm where he had worked as a teenager, before old man Odrek had sacked him for being too friendly with their granddaughter. The farm was right on the edge the Valle de Pedroches. The place was unoccupied, put in trust by the old man for a non-existent heir, there was a caretaker to look after the livestock that was left. But he was no problem to deal with. All would be well, he would take it and his horses would be happy there. Just one more deal and he would be done.

Rafael's legitimate businesses had done well and provided a cover for the less salubrious aspects, the latest of which was a money laundering operation for some Russian acquaintances. It had proved very lucrative, but hiding money was difficult these days with electronic tracking and money laundering rules. He had had to stretch his operation further than he would have liked to hide the proceeds.

The drugs were a different matter, they were smuggled in from Africa via his coffee import business and then distributed throughout Europe and hidden in the hams from the Cabanillos factory in Malaga. It was a risky business, the last shipment had been intercepted by the police in the UK and had caused havoc with his customers. There was always another criminal gang vying to take over the operation and this had not helped.

The Police would be unable to work quickly enough for Rafael to worry about the next shipment being picked up. It was taking a different route into the UK via Grimsby. The police wouldn't have time to trace it and organise a raid in such a short space of time.

Rafael had always managed to stay one step ahead and he was convinced that the shipment wouldn't be intercepted again. He had told his contacts to expect its arrival. It had to go as planned. He didn't trust the Russians and he didn't want to end up supporting the foundations of a new motorway.

Chapter 17

Marguerite was worried, she had woken from a nightmare she hadn't had for years. She was running, Rafael was following her but each time she thought she had found safety, he found her, and dragged her from her hiding place. She could not see his face, but she knew the shadow behind was Rafael.

Marguerite threw back the Chinese print duvet, got up and paced across the carpet of her bedroom. She had had a feeling of disquiet ever since the body of that young woman had been found. It had raked up a lot of fears and brought back memories that Marguerite had thought were long buried. She had been thinking about her brutal husband, whose memory she had blanked out as much as she could since her flight from their apartment in Madrid one rainy night over 30 years ago.

She took with her a couple of bruised ribs, marks all over her body and a black eye as a reminder of his brutality. The last straw had been when Marguerite discovered once again that she could not provide an heir to her husband's empire, of course he wouldn't accept it was because of the constant beatings he inflicted upon her. No, it was her fault, she was glad she did not have a child to be brought up with Rafael as a father. He had become more and more cruel over time and controlled her every move. He made her sit for hours on a hard chair in his office not moving. If she did, he would move across the room to stamp on her feet or slap her face or worse, he would do nothing, just look over at her with that cold expression she knew so well. She knew that he was storing up all the misdemeanours committed during a rare trip outside, until they arrived back at the apartment where he would be free to terrorise her as much as he wanted. He had beaten her so badly once, she took six months to recover. At the hospital, the doctors tried to get her to say what had happened, but fear made her say "I fell."

The attack had made her realise he would eventually kill her. It was then that she resolved to get away from him and started to plan her escape.

Since the first attack she had hidden her identity card and some cash with the small amount of jewellery her mother had left her. It was well hidden in a small alcove behind the shelves in her dressing room. Marguerite worried that her husband would discover her hiding place and this added to her anxiety. The night before she planned to leave, she heard him return home. She could gauge his mood by his footsteps and the way he closed the front door. He really did not need an excuse to beat her, he enjoyed having her under his control, the power of her being scared was the point of it all. She heard the door slam. Marguerite waited for him to call her. She dared not move from the floor in the corner of the room where he had told her to wait for his return. She waited, her hands shaking and her stomach churning. When he called, she stood, tried to make her legs come back to life and went quickly to the large living room to greet him.

"Why is my drink not ready you stupid woman?" he shouted. "Do you think I pay for your upkeep and then have to do everything myself?"

"Sorry" Was all she could manage to say.

She had learned long ago not to speak up, although whether she spoke or not, in this mood, his actions would be the same. Anything she did would give him his excuse. Marguerite almost ran to the decanter of fine brandy; her hand shook as she took out the stopper and watched in horror as it dropped to the floor. It rolled, in what seemed slow motion to Marguerite, coming to rest at her husband's boot. He looked at her, his face a mask of fury.

"If it was not this, it would be something else" she thought.

He crossed to Marguerite and slapped her hard across the right side of her face, she felt the sharp sting of his signet ring and fell with the power of it. She tried to get up, but before she could recover, he was on top of her, he lifted her dress and ripped her underwear, he roughly shoved his hand into her, she screamed.

"Oh no you don't." he whispered quietly into her ear. "No screaming, be silent now or it will be worse for you"

He turned her onto her stomach, forcing her head to the floor, her skull flattened against the tiles, she saw the pattern stretching away from her as he entered her roughly. Holding her down his left hand gripped her neck restricting the blood supply and making her dizzy. His other arm wrapped around her ribs to hold her firmly. Marguerite was too scared to fight back and feared that this time he may kill her.

Tears fell silently from her eyes onto the tiled floor as he lunged back and forth, when he had finished, he leaned back and used his fists to slam into her as he called her such terrible things.

When the attack was over, she lay curled in a ball, Rafael stood over her adjusting his clothing. Marguerite's mind and body was still blank with shock. She felt her hair being yanked backwards and Rafael pulling her up to her feet. He dragged her across the apartment to the kitchen. where he delivered a final kick to her backside and pushed her away from him. "Now, whore, get my dinner!"

She fell into the kitchen cabinets, bruising her already damaged ribs and fell to the floor. Marguerite lay still for a while gathering her clothes around her, tears streaming down her bruised face. It was not the first time this had happened, but she was determined that it would be the last.

Marguerite shakily managed to make and serve his dinner. Of course, he found fault with everything, how could she be expected to cook after such a traumatic attack?

"Stand behind me, woman, and don't move until I tell you." He growled as he began to eat.

She stood behind him not daring to move. He stood abruptly knocking the chair he was sitting on onto its back. He turned, grabbed the back of her neck and smashed her face into the dinner plate filled with the food she had just served.

"You don't expect me to eat this muck, do you? Now clear up bitch and you better be sitting on the floor in your place when I return, I'm going out." Then he left the room.

Chapter 18

Marguerite breathed shakily and her eyes darted to the door to make sure he was not playing a trick on her, waiting for her to move or leave the room. She heard the front door slam, and she was sure he wouldn't return until much later. Despite the suffering she had endured the thought of her escape gave her strength.

She hurried to retrieve her hidden possessions from the alcove in the dressing room, grabbed a coat and ran.

Once she was a safe distance away from the apartment in the up market and affluent Santander district of Madrid, Marguerite flagged down a cab and went to the bus station where she paid cash for a bus ticket to Malaga. She clasped her bag which contained all she had hidden over the past year. She had worried every day that her husband would discover her secret, but her luck had held out. He was too self-obsessed to think that she might have had any plans to leave him and was arrogant enough to think she would be too scared. She knew she would still have to be careful because he would look for her.

She vowed to do everything possible to make sure he didn't find her. Marguerite caught the 23:59 pm bus from Estacio Sur and slept most of the six-hour journey to Malaga.

Once in Malaga she stopped for a coffee and a pastry, receiving pitying looks from the counter staff and the other passengers at the bus terminal, she hoped that none of them would remember her if her husband came looking. She went to the cloakroom and tidied up her hair, a lady came in and offered her some foundation and lipstick to cover her bruises. Marguerite accepted them gratefully, thankful for the kindness of this stranger. The long bus ride gave her body a chance to rest, her ribs cried out with every movement, but she knew that the bruises would fade, her bruised mind would take longer. Surveying the result of her makeup, she left the cloakroom and caught another bus to Nerja, arriving in the seaside town just before mid-day.

Walking downhill from the bus station she felt a lightness in her spirit that she thought she would never feel again. She saw a shop called "Mariposas:" the name was painted in blue lettering on a white background with multi coloured butterflies and some tiny green leaves as a border. She needed to get her skirt repaired as she had not bought any other clothes with her. There was a notice in the window of the dress shop advertising for an assistant. Smoothing out the wrinkles in her clothing as best she could, Marguerite plucked up what little of her courage remained and went in to enquire about the job. The owner Senora Clemente sat at the counter, she was impeccably dressed in a pale-yellow dress with matching shoes, her grey hair was pinned back in a chignon. She was getting older and had been struggling to keep the shop going by herself. She took one look at the young woman with the black eye. Immediately took pity on her and offered her the job.

Something about Marguerite pulled at her heart strings. She looked up at the picture of her daughter Andrea that hung on the wall above the till and thought of what she would do if she were in the same situation as this young woman. Luckily, Andrea had married a good man and given her two beautiful grandchildren. So, she decided to offer Marguerite a room above the shop where she could stay until she got on her feet. Marguerite couldn't believe the kindness of this woman. It had been so long since someone had been nice to her, she began to cry. Senora Clemente reached beneath the counter and retrieved two glasses, a bottle of sherry and some tissues then poured Marguerite and herself a large measure to seal the deal.

Both Senora Clemente and Marguerite found the arrangement beneficial, Senora Clemente got a dependable assistant who could keep up to date with the latest fashion trends and was able to sew. Marguerite got a secure anonymous place to stay where she could try to forget about her tyrannical husband. As time went by, she confided in Senora Clemente who then left the running of the shop to Marguerite and spent her days sitting outside in the sun talking to her friends and passing the time with strolling tourists. Marguerite made the shop successful by stocking designer and everyday clothing in all sizes. Her customers brought fabrics to have skirts or blouses made up to a specific design. In time their profits rose, and Senora Clemente was able to completely retire, dropping in occasionally for a chat. Marguerite still had her jewellery and most of her cash in the bank as a safety net if she needed to get away again. She was able to manage her wages from the shop and had saved some money too.

One day Senora Clemente asked Marguerite if she would like to buy the shop from her, Marguerite had been running it successfully for years and it made perfect sense that she should have it. Despite this Marguerite was hesitant, she had always been free to leave if her husband ever caught up with her, buying the shop would mean putting down permanent roots. It had been fifteen years since she had left Madrid, no one had asked her about her past, she told everyone except Berta and Senora Clemente that she was a widow. Death was a great conversation stopper for most people and Marguerite was happy to leave the details aside. She told Senora Clemente that she would think about it. Marguerite loved the shops on the Calle Pintada. Her shop was near the Café Bar Las Quatro Esquinas, she was able to get churros and hot chocolate on the winter mornings and a fresh orange juice in the summer. The clothes shop had plenty of passing trade in the form of tourists enjoying the sun and lazily wandering the winding whitewashed streets. The locals also passed by on their way to the larger Mercadona supermarket in Calle San Miguel. One night just before closing a man entered the store acting very strangely, he told Marguerite he was shopping for a friend who knew her very well and would visit her soon. Then he left.

Marguerite's friendship with Berta had started when Berta, exasperated at the lack of larger sizes of clothes in the shops had bought some material to Marguerite to make up a dress for a party. Marguerite had done so and made the dress a very flattering shape. They talked easily for over two hours that first time. After that, their friendship was easy and long standing and they shared almost all their secret thoughts and fears, but Marguerite had never told her all the details about how brutal her husband, Rafael had been, she just said he was cruel.

Berta had been through some tough times since Juan had died in that terrible accident and Marguerite had been by her side, supporting Berta through her grief, she didn't want to burden her with more misery.

Marguerite told Senora Clemente about her visitor.

"I think you have certainly had a fright Marguerite." Senora Clemente consoled her.

"Surely he wouldn't send someone after all this time?"

"You know what he was like, I told you. I'm sure the man was sent to frighten me."

"I think you should go home and have a stiff drink and a good night's rest, you will see it more clearly tomorrow." Senora Clemente patted Marguerite's hand.

"You are right of course my dear Senora Clemente, I do know that whatever happens I'm not running, I love it here in Nerja. I have been very happy. I will go home and think it over. " "Maybe it was nothing."

Marguerite didn't settle that night until she had checked all the doors and windows were locked. She was sure Rafael had sent the man to frighten her, and that had worked, but she was determined not to let him take over her life again. If it was him, he would have a fight on his hands.

After a sleepless night or two she told Senora Clemente that she would buy her shop. Marguerite arranged to sell her mother's jewellery, apart from the small diamond ring she wore every day. Prices had increased considerably since she had inherited the gems and so together with her savings, she was able to afford to buy the shop. That was fifteen years ago, and she had never regretted her decision but now her old nightmares had returned, she hoped they were just the result of her imagination.

Chapter 19

Joe looked despairingly at the water dripping through the roof into the kitchen. He had repaired it so many times and now he was repairing the repairs. He wished he had the money to replace the entire roof, but it was just not possible. He thought back to when his mother was alive. For as long as he could remember there had only been the two of them. She had never talked about his father. Joe had never bothered trying to find out about him. They were happy on their little farm and didn't need anyone else.

Joe went into the dusty attic to look for the source of the leak so he could make a temporary repair. He looked around the cavernous, filled space; boxes were everywhere, mostly his mothers, but some were older. Joe knew he should start clearing it all out. Half of it was moth eaten and he was sure he had a family of bats in residence. Banging a shingle of wood over the latest hole to fill the gap Joe decided to look at some of the boxes. It was still raining. He had fed the pigs and done most of the other chores around the farm, so while he could find better things to do, he decided to look through the boxes. Old toys, clothes and games were first. He got slightly distracted upon finding his old Star Wars Millennium Falcon which had not been kept in its box or in a pristine condition. Joe remembered throwing it from the big oak tree in the field next to the house, hoping it would fly. But it just ended up with a chipped wing.

The next box he opened was filled with old curtains, The next with Christmas decorations, Joe didn't expect the lights would still work this year what with all the damp, even though he was on his own he still put up a tree and some decorations as he had done when his mum was alive, though they didn't make him feel as good as they had in those days. After spending a good couple of hours sorting boxes into two piles, one to keep and the other to get rid of, he lifted the nearest 3 boxes from the keeper pile and lowered them down through the loft hatch using the rope and pulley he had installed to help him move items in and out of the loft. Descending the ladder, he took the boxes into the kitchen and placed them next to the chair he kept by the wood burning stove. The wood burner had been his mother's idea, she had always loved the farmhouse kitchen and had had the burner installed so that she and Joe could sit and chat during the winter afternoons. Joe smiled as he thought of it, he could see his mum sitting with her cuppa, warming her toes. Joe sat on the opposite side and told her all about the pigs, the farm and his plans. Joe opened the first box. Old bills, receipts, insurance policies! Wait! thought Joe, what insurance? He opened the paper and saw it was an insurance policy for the contents of the house. Joe set it to one side and continued sorting. He burnt the old bills and statements as he went through and finally was left with a small pile of papers to read carefully. Joe opened the second box. He found some ornaments in this one, they had been carefully wrapped in tissue paper and were well padded against damage. Joe put this box to one side and opened the third. Joe found some documents that were written in a foreign language, he recognised that it was Spanish because his mother had written to her grandparents in Spanish, when they had been alive. Joe only knew English; he had never done very well at school. The words on the page always seemed to jump about when he was reading. His mum had found out he was dyslexic, and the school had helped but he had been fourteen by then and soon left school to work on the farm. He managed the bills and receipts etc but anything more complicated he got his friend Bill to help him.

Lastly, there was an ornate box containing more documents. Joe took these and put them with everything he had put aside on the table. Tomorrow he would take them to his friend Bill, who lived in Ipswich. They had been at school together. Bill had become a teacher and Joe a farmer. They had stayed friends and Bill had helped Joe a lot in the past with the more complicated paperwork he received from the Ministry of Agriculture and the EU. Joe trusted Bill completely and had relied on him heavily in the past.

Chapter 20

Rafael Cabanillos paced back and forth in his office. Another shipment was due out, but one of his men had really messed up by killing that young woman. Now the police would be all over the case and it would make his life more difficult. His Russian counterparts wouldn't be pleased, and they were not the type of people you wanted to annoy.

He pressed the intercom. "Andrea, send in Maria and Miguel."

"Si, Señor Cabanillos" came the reply.

The door opened immediately. Maria came in first. She wore a black suit jacket, white shirt and jeans. Her muscles strained at the seams of her trousers and jacket, her face was unlined apart from two lines on her jaw commonly associated with steroid abuse in body builders. Maria had spent many hours in the gym and had changed her diet adding anabolic steroids to enhance her shape. Unfortunately, this also increased her aggressive nature giving her a slightly masculine appearance. Rafael looked her over, she walked with the unease of a caged tiger. Maria was followed by Miguel, his sleek black hair pinned back like a flamenco dancer and his stick thin figure clothed entirely in black leather. He reminded Rafael of a poisonous serpent, his green eyes adding to the impression that he was just as deadly.

"I need you to go to the farm to make sure the drug storage is secure, and no-one is snooping about. I need to oversee the next shipment." Said Rafael "The locals have messed up and I want it done before the police come sniffing around. If we move fast, we will get this shipment out before they arrive. Go to the farm and make sure all is ready. I don't want any loose ends. I don't need to tell you that the shipment must leave on time. There are only a few days left so don't get it wrong!"

"We won't let you down Senor, we are always at your service." Maria smiled at Rafael and the look gave him a shudder because it was as if a wolf was eyeing him up for the kill. The smile didn't extend beyond her mouth, there were no laughter lines on her face or any other sign that she ever displayed any emotion. Rafael knew she was a formidable killer. Miguel said nothing as usual just stood behind Maria scanning the room with his hooded green eyes. He was always ready for trouble and was quick as lightning with the blade he carried. Rafael watched them leave the office and was glad this was his last big shipment. He looked forward to retirement and wouldn't miss the thugs he had had to work with over the years. He would make sure that Maria and Miguel were well looked after financially, so that they would be able to live as they wished and leave him alone once he retired. He admired their ruthlessness and efficiency but would rather not have them hanging around. He had purchased a villa for them in Rio de Janeiro. He was sure that in South America, they would be able to find plenty of human misery to keep them amused.

Rafael had found Maria and Miguel Guiterrez in a local children's home when they were both teenagers They had been placed there when their parents had abandoned them and their foster parents could no longer cope with their cruel ways, bullying other kids, being insolent and disruptive at school and at home and being arrested for shoplifting. The animal cruelty charges had been the last straw and the twelve-year-olds were once again taken into care by the authorities where they continued their reign of terror until Rafael provided them with a channel for their viciousness. Over the years they had worked hard for him and had put an end to many awkward situations. He had no doubt they would do whatever was necessary to make sure he was protected. They were the nearest thing he had to children, and they had showed him uncompromising loyalty in return.

Chapter 21

Elena returned to work, parking her moped in its usual spot. As she approached the building, her heart began to pound, she felt breathless, her eyes darted left and right, and the noises all around her seemed very loud. She felt the pain in her head again with an alarming sense of reality, leaning on the wall she took a moment to catch her breath. She was glad when she saw the concierge. sitting at his desk as usual. Elena passed through the barriers, she still felt shaky, she looked up and down the corridor leading to her office and jumped when she heard a noise from inside one of the other rooms, she had not realised the effect the attack had had on her, if only Jorge hadn't gone to the dentist that day she wouldn't have been attacked. Why she had been attacked she still didn't know, did Jorge have anything to do with it? No, surely not, he would never get mixed up in anything criminal, but Elena couldn't quite shake off the feeling of nervousness and she only began to breathe normally once she reached her office.

She saw Jorge through the glass door of her office. He had his feet on her desk, as he drank a fruit juice and ate an almond croissant, flakes from which were falling over the desk and all the files. He had come to work for the laboratory two years before, after achieving passable grades at college. Elena had often wondered how he had managed to get the job until she found out that he was the nephew of the recently elected Mayor. She had been upset to think that her boss would be pressured into taking a candidate because of his family ties. She had complained to him at the time, but he had just shrugged and told her to get on with it. Jorge managed the job quite well but was sometimes easily distracted and missed things like leaving evidence behind at the scene or forgetting to label evidence properly. Elena had given him some leeway and he had improved but he still had a long way to go before she would trust his work completely

"Elena!" he cried guiltily, sitting upright and pushing the chair backwards on its creaky wheels. "I didn't think you'd be back so soon."

"Well, that's obvious." Elena replied, "Would you get your feet off my desk and tell me what you have found so far?"

Jorge jumped up, spilling his juice on the floor, following up with more croissant crumbs. "Yes Elena, sorry" he mumbled. "I'll be back in a moment, sorry."

Elena watched Jorge cross the glass-walled office and sighed. He was a good worker if she were there to nag him. Elena wanted him to be better.

Elena read the report Jorge had produced, the DNA result from the tissue underneath the victim's fingernails had been returned while she was in hospital.

Elena was also glad they now had a definitive ID for the victim too, she liked to treat the bodies that came to her with respect and knowing their name helped with the process. With all the latest information at hand from Armando included by Jorge, she left the office and entered the changing rooms to don her sterile suit ready to work.

She knew that Armando was investigating and wanted to help him catch the culprit quickly.

If drugs were involved, then the police were on a tight timeframe to catch the criminals.

Elena wanted to re-examine the joint of ham and asked Jorge to bring it to her.

"I thought Armando would have told you." Jorge said nervously. "The ham joint is missing, I've looked everywhere. It must have been taken when you were attacked."

Chapter 22

Marguerite was crossing the Plaza De Canava to go to the Municipal restaurant where she volunteered to help with the old people's meals every Thursday. There was the usual number of tourists milling about along with others sitting outside the bars and restaurants, people watching. The coach parties that came to explore the whitewashed streets had not yet arrived. Marguerite stopped to admire the elegant pair of midnight blue shoes in a shop nearby as she had had her eye on them for a while and was in the process of deciding whether to buy. Over the years she had had to watch her budget. She had always implemented the three-day rule when thinking of buying something luxurious. This meant that if on day one she wanted to buy something expensive she waited three days, if she still wanted it after that, she would buy it. This meant that she sometimes missed out but had curbed her compulsion to impulse buy. As she looked at the shoes, she saw the reflection of a man in the window. For a moment she was too stunned to move but she knew who it was. She turned and looked at the back of the now retreating figure. Yes, she was sure it was him. That cocky walk, the angle he held his head. The now grey hair neatly cut. Rafael. She didn't know what to do first. Her heart was beating loudly in her chest, she felt the palms of her hands grow moist, her breathing became rapid, and she had to lean on the wall outside the newspaper shop to catch her breath. One of her neighbours passed by and asked if she was alright and she managed to stutter out a reply. Then staying close to the shop doorways, she finally reached the restaurant. Marguerite explained to the chef, Angela, that she wouldn't be able to stay and help today as she had a burst pipe at home and had to wait for the plumber to call.

Checking the street outside she left the restaurant, she turned back past the Kronox café, crossing the Balcon de Europa, and the souvenir shops at the corner of the Carabao and ran home. Once there she locked and bolted the door and paced the house, not knowing what to do next. Why was he here? Had he found her? After all these years, surely, he was not still looking for her?

Marguerite picked up the phone and dialled her friend Berta.

"What can I do Berta? I know it was him."

Berta knew Marguerite's story and had listened many times to her worries.

"There is only one thing to do Marguerite, and that is find that nice police officer and tell him everything. Only when that husband of yours is behind bars will you be able to rest easily." Marguerite was worried, but Berta was right.

She telephoned police headquarters in Malaga and asked for Officer Ramirez.

"I'm sorry Senora, Officer Ramirez is out on a case, I can take all the details from you and pass them to him.

Usually, these old ladies were just panicking over nothing, the police officer thought. The officer was taken aback when Marguerite's voice changed.

"I have told you I need to see Officer Ramirez. Tell Officer Ramirez to call me please as soon as he returns. It is very important." With that Marguerite replaced the receiver.

Chapter 23

Rafael knew the pain he had caused Marguerite. He had wanted her to see him and be frightened. The way she ran like a scared rabbit to her house had proved him right. He would deal with her later. He loved the feeling of power her fear gave him. He had booked into the Parador Hotel and was waiting for Maria and Miguel, his most trusted sidekicks, to let him know all was well at the farm and that it had been cleared of anyone causing a problem. He intended it to be his retirement villa, he had worked there as a teenager and had fun with the granddaughter too. He smiled when he thought of how he had terrified her. All the old buildings would be demolished, and no expense would be spared in rebuilding. The people who did the work for him owed him much and so they kept what they saw as a secret knowing that if they didn't it would mean their lives. He would go there later himself to make sure all was in order. He stood on the balcony of his room and surveyed the Burriana Beach and the sea below. "It is one of the best places in Andalusia," he thought. "When I'm settled there on my farm in the hills, I'll have the sea in front of me and the mountains at my back." The thought made Rafael smile a little. A niggling worm of doubt crept into his thoughts as he remembered the Russians who had fronted the transport links and men at the factory and their threats. Rafael suppressed the thought once more. I'm sure it will go smoothly, it is my last job, he thought.

Once cleared of all those old buildings, stables and a paddock would be built for his horses. Bridle paths would be cut into the forest. The pigs that roamed there would find themselves turned to ham a little prematurely. Nothing could be allowed to upset his plans.

Chapter 24

"Joe, wake up! Joe."

"Who is banging on the door? It is being banged like a barn door in a thunderstorm" thought Joe,

"Whatever is going on?"

"Joe, come on, hurry up, you need to see this" The voice shouted.

Joe pulled on a t-shirt over his boxers and went down the stairs, missing the creaky one as he always did, a habit kept from childhood. Opening the door, he found Bill, box in arms. Bill pushed past Joe and went straight into the kitchen. He looked as if he had had no sleep. His face was pale, his eyes had black rings underneath. "Blimey Bill, what happened to you? You look like a bedraggled cat! Come in I'll put the kettle on."

"You will not believe what is in amongst those Spanish papers you gave me to look at!" gasped Bill.

"Oh! What are they? Nothing important surely? What you talking about you daft h'apeth?" Joe scratched his head.

"These documents you gave me Joe, they are documents holding a farm in Spain in trust for you until your 50th birthday. You have to go to Spain to claim it or lose your inheritance."

"Bill, I think you might have had a stroke or something. I haven't got any money. Not even enough to get to Ipswich let alone Spain."

"Don't worry about that now Joe, Let's sit down, and I will go through it all with you."

Joe followed Bill to the kitchen, pulled out the wooden kitchen chair, scraping the flagstone floor with a nasty screech and trying to make sense of what Bill was telling him.

Spain? What did he know about Spain? If only his mum had told him more of her story, he might find it easier to understand what on earth was happening?

Still confused Joe made the tea and handed a cup to Bill, then sat down.

"The first thing I came across was this."

Bill held out a large document with the seal of a government office on it and lots of writing in Spanish.

"This is a deed to a farm in Andalusia, which is a province in southern Spain. It shows that your great grandfather had a farm there that reared Iberico pork for ham. I looked it up and it seems the pigs roam free in the acorn forests and then are sold for their meat which depending on the quality can be worth a lot of money. Anyway, Joe, that is not the important part of the story."

"The farm was passed to your grandfather and after his death to your mother. She was settled in England by that time and had you to look after and so your grandfather placed the property in trust for her or her descendants. That is you!"

"Well, I knew I had Spanish blood in my family but never would have guessed all this Bill." Joe sat back in his chair looking mystified. "It's a good job you know what it means."

"What it means! What it means! What it means my old pal is that you own a pig farm in Spain and if you don't go and claim your inheritance soon the government will get it!! I will help you get started."

"First, we need to find a lawyer for you, one that knows about inheritance and property laws and next we need to get you a flight to Spain and ask Fred Moffatt, next door to look after your pigs. Ready?"

Joe wasn't sure he was ready but nodded his head in agreement.

Chapter 25

When the night security guard had passed Maisie ran across the yard to the loading bay. Rolling under the plastic door strips she checked her presence had not been detected before crossing to the stairs. As she came to the top of the stairs, Maisie checked once more that the night security guard had not changed his routine then quickly crossed the corridor to the Administration offices. She went first to Senor Fernandez's office and began to search his large oak desk. Starting with the bottom drawer.

When she had first joined the police, an old burglar she had arrested told her that it was a mistake to start looking in the top drawer in a cabinet, it wasted time because you had to slide one drawer in to look in the next one down. If you started at the bottom, you could leave them all open until you reached the top and then close them all at once or not. She went through the papers inside the bottom drawer, nothing out of the ordinary. She moved to the next drawer up; nothing there. She opened the top drawer. It was stiff on the runners and Maisie had to pull harder to release it. The drawer suddenly released and came clear of the desk, spilling the contents onto the floor. Maisie froze waiting for the sound of approaching footsteps, she hoped it had not made too much noise. She went through the papers hastily putting them back into the drawer before lifting it into place, just as she did she noticed something stuck to the underside of the desk above the drawer. Reaching in she retrieved the envelope that was stuck there. She unfolded the paper and found a list of shipments, the next one scheduled for five days' time, destination. Grimsby. Masie pocketed the list and replaced the drawer, closing them all carefully she left the office.

Back in the loading bay she noticed a crate in the area she had seen the suspicious characters milling about. She didn't have time to think, she ran over to the crate, peeled back the covering. Inside were legs of ham packed together. Maisie knew that this was how the drugs had been transported to Ipswich when the shipment had been intercepted. She lifted out a joint of ham. It was heavy and Maisie had some difficulty getting a secure hand hold on it. She found some rope in the corner of the bay and made a makeshift handle to attach to the ham, so that she could carry it more easily, a trick her dad taught her for carrying firewood on one of their many camping trips. Looping the ham over her shoulder she checked the coast was clear, left the factory and returned to her car. Sliding into the driving seat she drove quickly away from the factory, pleased that her visit had gone well. When she got back to the apartment, she would record everything she had found so that she could pass it to the authorities in Malaga.

A black 4 x 4 followed at a safe distance; the headlights dimmed. The driver had done this sort of work many times so knew how to remain unseen.

When she got back to her apartment Maisie put the ham on the small table. She would figure out what to do in the morning. She knew her boss, Inspector Last would be angry when he found out that she had gone to Spain, not to rest but to investigate the drug supply line. She hoped her results would save her from dismissal.

Maisie suddenly realised how tired she was and after a quick shower, went to bed. A noise woke her. Checking her phone, she saw it was 3.30am. The hotel maids and cooks started working at that early hour and they were often chatting noisily in the street, however, this noise, Maisie was sure, had come from inside the apartment. Slipping on her green shoes, as they were the nearest, she got up slowly and went to the bedroom door. She saw a man's figure going through her bag. She picked up the nearest weapon she could, which was the leg of ham and held it out in front of her.

"What are you doing here" she shouted. "Get out"

The man turned, he was large, it seemed his head was welded directly on to his shoulders. he looked like he had spent a lot of time in the gym. He moved towards Maisie, grabbing her round the waist, she tried to use the ham to hit him but dropped it. She reached up and scratched his face, he yowled with pain and dropped her, she fell heavily hitting her head on the TV cabinet by the balcony door. Maisie tried to get up, but her vision was blurred, and she could feel blood running down the side of her face. Her left hand scrabbled for a weapon, but there was nothing to grab. The man placed his hands around her neck, she looked into his cold eyes seeing the tattooed teardrop underneath, as panic started to set in. Maisie kicked and tried all the self-defence techniques she had learnt at police college, He didn't loosen his grip, he was far too strong, her eyes closed. She felt him pick her up, in one arm, opening the balcony door with the other. As he walked towards the balcony, he kicked the ham out of his way, and it went flying to the ground below. Maisie weakly hit his arm with hers, she became dizzy and could not think clearly. Still too weak to fight him off Maisie struggled and felt panic set in as he manoeuvred her to the balcony railing. She grabbed futilely at his clothes, her head was spinning as her eyes flickered and closed, she had a fleeting vision of her mum's face, then she felt nothing but air beneath her, then darkness came. The man looked briefly over the edge of the balcony. He saw the ham lying beside the body. He should go and retrieve it but couldn't take the risk of someone spotting him. He had already made a considerable amount of noise. He returned to the job of finding anything that Maisie may have taken from the factory, he worried what the boss would say when he heard about the girl. He turned out the entire room but could not find anything. He took her laptop and her phone and left the building undetected to return to his car. He would worry about the girl later. Moving stealthily across the marble tiled corridor he congratulated himself on getting rid of the woman, one less obstacle in the way. A job well done. The thought of the joint of ham nagged at the back of his brain, but he decided he might be able to retrieve it later or maybe he would keep its existence to himself. He guessed that forensics would retrieve it and then he would be able to get it back.

Chapter 26

Joe and Bill worked all day, searching the internet for a flight to Malaga that landed at a reasonable hour. The first available flew from Stanstead to Malaga at 10.15 the next morning and landed at 1.15pm Spanish time.

Bill searched for an English-speaking Spanish inheritance and property lawyer. He settled on Antonia Munoz, from her picture she looked like a mature no-nonsense person. Her website was very professional and able to be read in Spanish and English. There were many good reviews from previous clients. Joe spoke to her secretary, and she was able to confirm that Antonia was an expert with Spanish property and inheritance laws and would be able to meet Joe. She had a free appointment on the day after he arrived and so the appointment was made for 10am.

Bill booked a hotel for Joe, near the offices of Antonia Munoz in the old quarter of Malaga. Joe raided his savings, The roof would have to wait. Bill said he could loan him the rest of the money he needed for fares and hotels. He would also pay for Antonia Munez's fee. Joe could pay him back when everything was sorted.

"Bill, are you sure? It's a fair bit of money and you've already helped me so much."

"Don't worry Joe, I'll be looking for a free holiday in Spain every year after this, now don't mention it again. What are friends for?"

Next Joe went to see his neighbour, Fred Moffat. Fred always looked after Joe's livestock if Joe was away or if he had to go with his mum to her hospital appointments. After relaying the amazing story of Joe's inheritance Fred said he was more than happy to feed and look after the pigs on the farm for Joe. He could start the next day as long as Joe had enough feed and bedding in stock.

Joe phoned the feed merchant and ordered all he needed for at least three weeks so Fred wouldn't need to order anything extra.

Chapter 27

Armando waited in the arrivals area of Malaga airport for Inspector Last of the Suffolk Constabulary, His name was written on the card that Armando held in front of him. It was a particularly sticky day, and he was slowly losing his cool disposition. He could feel the rivulets of sweat running down his back as he sweltered under the cloudless skies that reflected in the glass roof of the arrival lounge. He watched the travel weary passengers file past him and meet taxi drivers and relatives.

Finally, Armando saw a man of about 50, checked shirt untucked from his jeans, navy jacket with shiny lapels that looked like it had seen better days, and scuffed brown deck shoes. The man's face was a bright shade of pink as he mopped his profusely sweating brow. He pulled a small suitcase with a tick on one side and a picture of Fireman Sam on the other that looked like it had been rescued from a child. The man walked straight up to Armando, hand outstretched.

"Officer Ramirez I presume?" he smiled and immediately his face lit up changing it completely. His brown eyes crinkled at the edges and his mouth turned up in a wide grin. "Gosh, that was a journey. Just about room for me behind in that budget airline seat. still, I'm here now, Detective Inspector Bob Last, Suffolk CID." He shook Armando's hand firmly. "Shall we get on then Officer, I haven't got long here and would like to find out what happened to my colleague, damn fine police officer she was too. Tragic!"

Armando had not been able to squeeze in a word yet and was happy to have the opportunity to direct Detective Inspector Last to the car.

"My colleague Karim El Baz will meet us at the station, and we will have a full briefing then. I'm sure you must be weary after travelling, I will take you to your hotel first to freshen up if that's OK with you?"

"Thanks, I will just drop my bag off and be straight down. No time to lose. My chief will be mad as hell if I break the budget"

True to his word, Bob Last was back within an hour, Armando had waited in the air-conditioned, chic lobby of the hotel glad of the chance to keep cool. They began the drive from the airport to the police headquarters in Plaza Manuel Azaña travelling along the Ctra. Ronda Oeste passing the Parque Epressarial business park on the left and the Parque de los Esepedrolos on the right. Negotiating the one-way system at Santa Cristina and proceeding along the Avenue de Blas Infant, parking in the Calle Conan Doyle, so named because the great man had once visited Malaga and of course for his connection to law enforcement via his great detective Sherlock Holmes.

Bob Last seemed relieved to get out of the car and Armando had seen him grimacing and gripping the seatbelt tightly on the journey. He smiled secretly to himself, he loved to drive fast and having a police car was the perfect excuse. Armando was used to scaring his passengers. Sometimes when they got to headquarters, they were happy to confess to their crimes if it meant they wouldn't have to get in Armando's car again.

"Well, you certainly know the roads, Officer, I'll give you that, but I find it strange being on the wrong side of the road!"

"Please call me Armando, I don't think we need to be too formal. Also, I think you will find it is you who drive on the wrong side of the road." Smiling, Armando held the door open for Bob to enter the station.

Karim was waiting for him in the office, his long limbs dangling as he perched on the edge of the desk, twitching with nervous energy while his large brown eyes scanned the room. After the introductions had been made Armando went through what they knew about the case so far. Elena had joined them. Elena pointed to the picture of Maisie Bright in the middle of the whiteboard and began, "Miss Maisie Bright was murdered on Saturday night, cause of death was the impact from the fall, however there were bruises around her neck to show she was partially strangled before being thrown from the balcony whilst still alive. She also had marks on her wrists and defensive wounds on her hands, and bruises on her midriff. She put up quite a fight. She had tissue under her fingernails, and this was sent for DNA analysis. I have just received the results thanks to my friend Paulo in that department. Karim stood up. "Here is Denikin Yakov Mikhailovich" displaying a mug shot of a crop headed man with a teardrop tattoo under his right eye.

"I know him" said Inspector Last "He's also known as Yasha the Basher. He's wanted in the UK for various things like extortion, torture, kidnapping, drug running."

Karim picked up the photo from the desk and pinned it to the board. A tough looking man peered out at them through small eyes and a scar running from his lips to his hairline on the left side and a tattoo of a teardrop under his right eye.

"He is a low-level muscle man for the Remizov family, who are well known for drug running and many other illegal activities. If the Remizovs are involved, then this is a big operation. Bigger than we can manage Armando. We should let the serious crime department deal with it." Suggested Karim.

"I'm not about to hand this case over yet. It happened on our watch, and I feel a responsibility to carry it through. This young woman did not deserve to be murdered and I intend with your help to find the killer and bring him to justice." He watched his team and was glad to see that they were all eager to do the same.

"I know it will mean a lot of hard work over the next few days, but Maisie Bright deserves the best we can give. I will liaise with the serious crime squad to get some back up should we need it."

"What about the joint of Ham that was found, did that tell us anything Elena?" said Armando returning to his chair.

"The joint of Ham found in the alley, contained 0.5 kg of cocaine. Hidden inside a plastic bag inside a pouch cut into the thickest part of the meat. The supplier was Odreck Ham, a farm up in the hills. They supply the Cabanillos factory in Malaga. Of course, this is only from my memory seeing that the evidence was stolen from my laboratory." Elena sat down.

"Thank you, Elena, Inspector Last, Bob, do you have anything for us?"

Inspector Last stood up, he was used to giving these briefings but had never had to do so to a Spanish audience, he was glad that they all spoke English as his Spanish vocabulary only extended to ordering a beer.

"Detective Bright was one of our best officers and her death has come as a great shock to my colleagues and to me. I worked with her closely and am sorry that this has happened to her. She was a brilliant police officer." Bob stood a moment gathering his thoughts with his head bowed, he could see Maisie's face on the board and felt both sadness and anger.

"This case started in Suffolk," he continued "After a shipment of ham laced with cocaine was seized in Ipswich but we couldn't trace it back further. We then found that the pork came from a farm in the hills on the way to Cordoba, er…. Viajes Valle de Los Pedroches,"

Last consulted his notebook for this last piece of information.

"Is this why Officer Bright was in Spain, Inspector?" asked Armando

"No, no she was on leave, she had an injury at work and needed to rest. Also, her brother died last year from a drug overdose, and she had become obsessed with finding the dealers. She had been working on her days off and at weekends and was burnt out, I had told her to keep out of it, leave it to the drug squad, but it was affecting her work in the department and so when she asked for leave after the attack on her, I granted her request. I had no idea she would come to Spain."

Armando pushed his chair back impatiently.

"You should have asked for my help sooner, Inspector Last, we should have been told of the shipment of drugs when it arrived in Ipswich. It was from my patch after all."

"We did report it, of course, to the chief of the police department of Andalusia. I thought you would have been told." replied Bob

Armando looked down hoping that the Inspector wouldn't see his consternation at the thought that someone in his organisation may have withheld information.

Bob, noting the change in the way he was addressed, said simply.

"I wish I could go back."

With that his voice cracked and he turned his face away from them all and dabbed his eyes with a handkerchief.

"We don't have time to go over and find out the 'what happened was' of it all." said Karim "We have a killer and a drug shipment to find before the next consignment leaves, regrets are a waste of time and energy, let's focus on the enemy."

"I found a list in Constable Bright's apartment and the next shipment from the factory goes on Saturday. We have a lot to do before then. So far, the only evidence we had was the Ham joint stuffed with drugs that was stolen from the lab, Maisie's body and a list of shipments. But now we know from the DNA results that this Mikhailovich guy is her murderer."

"I will liaise with the serious crime squad to send a team to the factory on Saturday night and stop any shipments leaving. I will get Dominguez to research the owners of the factory and the farm and see if we turn up anything more.

Karim and I will go to the farm tomorrow to see if we can add any information to what we already have. You can come with us Bob, but you must stay out of any action."

Armando reached for the telephone, speaking rapidly told his boss Martin Jerez, all that had happened and his plans for solving the mystery of Maisie Bright's death and the drug trafficking from the Ham farm and factory.

After that Armando spoke to Mateo de la Fuente, head of the serious crime squad, and gave him a brief outline of the plans. He would hold a further meeting on Saturday morning at 7am to finalise the raid.

"I will send two of my guys to keep watch at the factory before then and gather as much information as we can." Mateo said

"Thanks Mateo, I know your guys are professional and reliable and I certainly owe you a nice cool beer after this."

When the meetings and planning had taken place, Armando drew Karim to one side. "Karim, try to find out who took the message about the drug shipment, but keep it between us for now."

Chapter 28

Joe arrived at Malaga airport and looked for a taxi driver Bill had booked for him. He should have his name on a card. The foyer was full of people coming and going. The first thing that struck Joe, was the light, the sun streamed through the windows and glass ceiling. Joe marvelled at the palm trees he could see swaying outside as he passed through another door where many drivers were waiting for their customers with names on cards held in front of them. Joe searched for his name and saw a rather large dark-haired man in white shirt and baggy trousers holding a card with JOE ODRECK written on it.

"Hello, I'm Joe Odreck" he said holding out his hand.

The man looked down and said "Come this way. Did you have a good journey?" in the broadest Yorkshire accent Joe had ever heard.

"Yes thanks," said Joe. Relieved the man spoke English.

On the way to the hotel, they chatted about football and England and the weather of course. Joe was amazed when the journey was over.

"If you need owt else, give us a call." Mike Clarke the card said.

"Thanks Mike, I will." said Joe.

Joe entered the hotel, it was decorated in the style of the Moors, coloured tiles and small wooden window frames around a central courtyard with stairs winding up to the higher floors. He approached the desk and booked into his room. The sand-coloured stone of the walls of the old city of Malaga reflected the late afternoon light into the room.

He could hear the hum of tourists passing by the window in the street below. He freshened up and after giving the paperwork a quick glance he decided to explore Malaga old town and get some dinner. His hotel was in the Calle Alamos, he asked at the hotel reception if they knew of a restaurant that served plain Spanish food. He also asked what was nearby for him to see. He left the hotel with the name of the Restaurant Cortijo Pepe, and the directions to the Alcazaba de Malaga, an ancient castle left from the invasion of the Moors. Joe enjoyed his dinner of mixed seafood and salad, washed down with a glass of cool Spanish beer. Joe wandered along the street passing restaurants full of tourists eating and drinking,

Different aromas reached him as he passed, Paella, gambas, and beer. How nice, he thought, to be able to sit outside in the evening and watch the world go by without the aid of 5 jumpers, wellingtons and a rain mac.

He turned into the Calle Alcazabilla and saw to his left the Roman theatre, it was below pavement level and Joe could clearly see the amphitheatre seating tiered before the central stage. He turned down a small walkway and found a set of steps leading to the Mirador de Alcazaba. Breathing heavily as he reached the top he was rewarded with a view from the top of the city and beyond it the pale blue Mediterranean. Joe stood and felt something within him rise to the surface. A feeling of déjà vu, a sense of belonging. He suddenly felt as if he had come home to Spain!

It was amazing, he had always thought of himself as Suffolk born and bred but now the sense of coming home hit him like a train. He had never been one to believe in all that new-fangled stuff about past lives, reincarnation etc, but standing here on the Mirador surveying Malaga and beyond he felt strangely calm. He returned to his hotel the same Joe, but somehow changed.

The next morning Joe was more than ready to meet Antonia Munoz. The sun had risen over the Mediterranean, and he could feel the heat developing into another sweltering day. Almost as soon as he arrived Antonia started to explain about his inheritance and suddenly Joe was in a whirlwind of paperwork, he signed his name so many times, he lost count.

After 2 hours and a cup of coffee and some sweet rolls Antonia held out her hand and spoke. "And now you are the owner of the farm of your ancestors. Congratulations. My secretary will lodge these papers with the relevant authorities, and we shall have some lunch. Tomorrow we will go and see the farm itself. I arranged for a surveyor to make sure the land and buildings match the deeds and I expect his report later this afternoon. I will pick you up at 10 am in the morning."

"Thank you, Senora Munoz. For everything. "Joe said

"Mr Odreck, I will take you. There are a few checks I need to make to finalise the paperwork, an inventory of buildings and livestock and land. To make sure all that is in the deed is included. You don't want your neighbours paring off parts of it for their own use. I have asked a surveyor to meet us there."

Joe headed back to his hotel. Once in his room he stretched on the bed, his brain ticked over with all the marvellous happenings of the last few days. It was almost too much. "Oh mum!" he sighed "I wish you had told me."

Chapter 29

The next morning Antonia was waiting. Joe got into the passenger seat, strapped on his seat belt, and they were off. Antonia took the more picturesque route to the Valle de Pedroches. As they drove through El Chorro, a small town frequented by hillwalkers and climbers, Antonia began to tell the story of the inheritance and how it would now pass to Joe. "Your great grandfather felt strongly that a male relative should inherit the farm, he felt so sad that your grandmother had gone to England, but he knew she was in love with an Englishman. They missed her terribly. And when she and your grandfather were killed, and your mother was sent to Spain to live with them they hoped she would stay. But she didn't and so your great grandfather always hoped that his great grandson would return and run the farm again. "

"I'm afraid that since your great grandparents' time the farm has suffered a little from lack of investment, the surveyor was satisfied that the deeds are correct, but he couldn't gain access to the house as the gate was locked and a large dog was guarding it. He managed to assure me the house is entire and liveable though it does need renovating. However, the herd of pigs are in fine health. They eat only acorns in the forest and their skin is black, the flesh has a high fat content which helps with the curing and gives it a unique flavour. I understand you are a pig farmer in England Joe?"

"Yes, I breed Saddlebacks and some Tamworth's. You would love the pigs. They have such a fantastic temperament, so easy to handle. They are rare breeds, so I get a good price for them at market. Of course, the house could do with some repairs, but I'm there by myself."

"Ahh Joe, now here is one of the best tapas restaurants in the whole of Spain, we will stop for a snack and then finish our journey."

Over a delicious "snack" of Padron peppers, chorizo cooked in sherry, croquettes of ham and chicken and bread, olives and olive oil, they chatted until Joe finally sat back and said "That was some snack, Antonia. If I keep eating like this, I'll be as fat as one of my pigs!"

Antonia told Joe more about the farm as she drove.

"I haven't been there myself but am told it is in a very secluded part of the valley, it's about 34 hectares, that's about 85 acres. It's mostly forest and meadows. The house itself is set into the hillside with a large living area and 5 bedrooms. There are also a number of outbuildings.

Someone made an offer for the farm recently but was told that it had been passed down the family. I understand they were not best pleased, but nothing can be done about that now. I got the feeling that the bidder was used to getting his own way."

The A45 wound its way uphill towards Cordoba, they passed through the town of Montilla, a large town with its own industrial park. Joe marvelled at the landscape of browned vegetation and almond trees. It was so different from the greenery of Suffolk. the heat shimmered off the road ahead creating a mini mirage and Joe had never felt more settled.

"I know it sounds a little silly Antonia, but since I went walking in Malaga over the last couple of evenings, I really feel as if I'm home. Do you think I'm going mad? I know my great grandparents and grandmother were Spanish, but I never really felt part of it before now."

Antonia pulled to the side of the road just before the farm, beneath them the land stretched away towards the sea, if they went on, they would reach Cordoba.

"Joe, you are a son of Spain, it is in your blood, the land of Andalusia runs through your veins. I think a part of us retains the sense of our origins and when we return it evokes a passion within us that we cannot always explain. All I can say is welcome home." She smiled and restarted the car and after another ten-minute drive they reached the gates of the farm with a name plate, Tierra de Paz (land of peace).

Chapter 30

Marguerite was alone in her house, she was still shaken by the package she had received and felt tired and upset. She lay down on her sofa and soon her eyes closed. She was transported to a night club in Malaga, she had gone there with her friends to celebrate a birthday. She felt full of energy and danced vigorously until her feet cried out for mercy. She was sitting in a plush velvet lined booth, massaging her aching feet after freeing them from her stiletto's when a handsome man approached her and handed her a drink.

"Here Senorina, I am sure you are thirsty after all that dancing" he whispered.

"Yes, thank you, I am but my father has warned me about taking drinks from strangers in clubs, it may contain what he called a Mickey Finn." she replied smiling.

"Very well," he held up his hand and called for a waiter. "An unopened bottle of champagne for the senorita por favor"

They laughed then and Marguerite thought he was charming. When the bottle came Rafael opened it with a flourish and poured her a generous glass. The pop of the champagne cork woke her from her siesta and she continued thinking about how terrible life with Rafael had been from the moment he married her.

He took her home that night and left her at the door with a chaste kiss on the cheek like a proper gentleman.

Of course, she said yes when he wanted to see her again.

During their courtship he behaved like a true gentleman, taking her to dinner and to the theatre. As their courtship went on he said he only needed her company if she suggested going out with friends and soon all her friends had drifted away to get on with their own lives.

They married in secret without even telling her parents and Rafael took her to Madrid. He did not let her work saying that no wife of his was going to work for others.

Gradually, over the first couple of months he took control of her life, dictating what she should wear, where she could go and to be available for him whenever he wanted her.

The first time she had objected to not being able to meet an old school friend for lunch he had hit her. Of course, he had been so, so, sorry and she had forgiven him. It must have been her own fault.

When she didn't get pregnant, he started to bully her relentlessly. He stripped away whatever self-esteem she had and turned her into the classic battered wife. She was scared of him, his temper was very volatile. She began to try and pre-empt his demands to keep him happy, but nothing was ever good enough.

Even when she had been injured so badly and he had taken her to hospital she just said she fell down the stairs. She knew the Doctor didn't believe her.

Finally, she had plucked up the courage to run. Now she was reliving the nightmare once more.

Chapter 31

The gate to the farm was locked with a chain and padlock. Behind the gate a large dog of indeterminate breed was straining at the end of a metal leash, snarling and barking at their arrival. Antonia looked a little puzzled, as an unfriendly looking man approached them.

"Que!" he barked.

"This is Joseph Odreck the owner of this farm, he has come to see his property, open this gate at once. Where is Paulo the manager?"

"He is having a little siesta, so vamoose Senora." the man rubbed a hand across his stubbled chin as if he had better things to do. Behind him someone dressed in black went into the house carrying a shotgun.

Joe was becoming more and more alarmed. He didn't like the look of this bloke or his dog for that matter.

"Maybe we ought to go and come back later." he suggested tugging at Antonia's arm, but she wouldn't be put off.

"Who is that? Who are you? What are you doing here? I'm calling the police now if you don't identify yourself and prove you have permission to be here" Antonia continued. This routine usually intimidated people and had the desired effect, but this man was not moving.

Antonia took her phone from her bag; the man opened the gate and came out. Joe was shocked by the speed with which he moved and took an involuntary step back. The man snatched the phone from Antonia, dropped it on the ground and crushed it with his boot. He pulled a gun from his waistband and directed them to walk in front of him. It didn't seem like a good idea to refuse. Joe and Antonia walked ahead.

"I'll take you to your amigo." he smirked as he shoved them through the door to a barn with a sloping corrugated roof at the back of the farmhouse. They saw something lying in the middle of the floor covered with a tarpaulin.

The corrugated iron sheeting on the roof looked as if it had seen better days and Joe could see the sky through some of the holes in it. He also noticed that termites had begun to erode the wooden beams holding up the roof. 'This barn is old and needs replacing' thought Joe, 'It's in a worse state than the one at home but of course his barn was made of English oak not flimsy, whatever this was.'

The man was joined by a woman dressed in a suit and carrying an automatic weapon. There were five wooden beams stretching along the front part of the barn, supporting the roof. Joe felt a hand shove him in the back making him stumble. Antonia grabbed his wrist after she was treated in the same way. The woman pushed them roughly until their backs were against the wooden columns as the man tied their hands and feet with strong rope,

Joe watched the pair, noting their hard eyes and ruthless looks. Antonia continued to protest but the second man hit her across her face to silence her.

"Quiet Abuela," he laughed. Walking over to the tarpaulin the man caught hold of the corner and flicking it back he uncovered a man's body,

"Here is your Amigo Abuela, but he is a bit quiet now as you can see. If you don't want to join him, shut up."

Joe and Antonia looked at the body of Paulo, blood had spread from his torso across the barn floor. Antonia turned her head away from the awful sight and looked across at Joe.

"Rafael Cabanillos owns this farm now. You see, you never arrived here. The trust your great grandfather setup will lapse and Senor Cabanillos, as always, will get his way. They will never find your bodies." Laughing the man walked to the door.

Joe was shocked, his brain went into overdrive, filled with questions.

"What had they walked in on? Who was this Cabanillos bloke? What were they doing on his farm?" Joe looked at Antonia's face streaked with tears and noted the look of defiance still in her eyes.

Paulo had been looking after the farm and its livestock for many years, producing some of the best ham in the area. He had been paid by the trust set up by Joe's ancestor and worked to keep it going until an heir came to claim his inheritance.

"Antonia, we will get out of here. I promise." Joe whispered as the pair left the barn locking the door behind them. "I didn't come all this way to be killed in my own barn!"

Chapter 32

Armando, Karim and Bob Last set off for the farm. With Armando driving they arrived in the late afternoon. Armando stopped the car well out of sight of the farm and retrieved his binoculars from the boot to look at the gate. It was locked with a heavy chain and padlock.

"Karim, see if there's another entrance, we don't want to announce our arrival, it looks fairly quiet, but we don't know what awaits us. Bob, you stay here, I can't be responsible for another British police officer getting hurt. I will come back for you when I know what's going on. If you hear gunfire, then call in for back up."

Bob, disgruntled at these instructions, tried to argue, but Armando's face told him that he was in no mood for discussion.

"Okay." he groaned "Who do I ring for help if you don't come back?" Karim had already disappeared along the fence line to the back of the farmhouse. Armando cautiously approached the front gate. He rattled it loudly. Armando waited but no-one appeared. A large rottweiler dog appeared from a kennel and began to bark. It strained at the long-chained leash that kept it from roaming free and jumped forward on its muscular hindquarters baring its saliva dripping teeth. Armando climbed over the gate and jumped down on the other side. He fixed his stare on the dog and began to talk to it. "Oye perro, ¿que es todo el ruido? ¡Siéntate! ¡Tranquilo! (Hey Dog, what is all the noise; sit down! Be quiet!)

Armando repeated the words over and over as he approached the barking animal; the dog's ears pricked up and surprisingly he sat with a sigh, then lay at Armando's feet, looking up adoringly.

"Good dog." said Armando reaching out to scratch the dog's ears.

Armando crossed the yard to the house. He found a blue bag on the table and on opening it saw it was full of a white powder. There were dishes in the sink and cigarette ends all over the floor along with beer cans and other rubbish.

Armando ventured upstairs and saw that one of the bedrooms was in use, the bed was unmade, and the room smelt of mould and dust. Cobwebs hung from the ceiling and Armando suddenly smiled as he thought of the expression on the apartment cleaner, Sofia's face, if she had been confronted with such a mess.

He made a quick search of all the rooms and was leaving the house when he saw Karim on the far side of the yard at the door to an old slope roofed barn. He had drawn his gun and was signalling to Armando to approach with caution. At the entrance Armando stood to one side while Karim kicked the door open, immediately Armando entered the doorway and scanned the room, his handgun at the ready. He saw two figures tied to the wooden beams, their heads spun round as Armando approached, Antonia breathed a sigh of relief when she saw them.

"What happened, who did this to you?" Armando said as he untied the ropes.

"Paulo, the farm manager is dead, there" gasped Antonia "Get Joe free too, hurry"

Karim stooped over the tarpaulin in the middle of the barn and flicked back its corner just as the bad guy had done. Armando untied Joe and made both him and Antonia sit down on some hay bales. "Wait there, I will get Inspector Last to come in too."

Chapter 33

"No, I don't think so, officer, you will sit beside the Abuela (grandma) and him." Armando turned and saw a woman holding an automatic weapon.

"Put down your gun officer, do not try anything. You too." She signalled to Karim with a flick of her gun.

Armando turned and saw Maria wearing her signature suit jacket, white shirt and jeans. She was closely followed by Miguel, his stick thin figure clothed in black leather. Armando knew them at once, Miguel and Maria Gutiérrez, they were infamous criminals, their picture had been on the wall of the police headquarters for a long time, but they always seemed to evade capture, they never left a witness alive. Armando knew he would have to think of something quickly if they were all going to get out in one piece. He was annoyed with himself for not leaving Karim to watch out for anyone approaching.

Miguel tied each of them to a beam in the barn, the rope was rough and old, and Miguel was not gentle. Armando felt the rough cord cut into his wrist.

"Maria and Miguel Gutierrez. How strange that you should be here. What evil business have you been carrying out this time? I've seen the drugs. Where's the boss?"

"He'll be along to claim his farm, don't you worry Officer. You and your companero's should not think about these things as you will not be around much longer." Maria's voice was dry and cracking like brittle greaseproof paper.

"This is my farm!" shouted Joe "My great grandfather left it to me! Get out and leave us alone!" Miguel stepped over and punched him in the stomach. Joe spluttered and coughed with the pain.

"Shh." Miguel held up one hand in front of Joe's face. "Our boss will be here soon, otherwise I would like to make you join our silent friend. I would enjoy that greatly." Joe looked into Miguel's eyes and had no doubt that his threat was real. He lowered his head, shuffled his feet and stared at the bottom of the wooden column he was tied to. Miguel stalked away to join his sister.

"Miguel, go and get ready," Maria ordered. Miguel left the barn. He did not ask "Get ready for what?"

The twins had a sixth sense when it came to communicating with each other. Maria, meanwhile, kept her weapon trained on the captives. She did not speak but paced back and forth as if she were a wild animal at the zoo waiting to be fed. Karim looked over at Armando and as Maria turned her back to him and shared a look that said, "What now?"

After what seemed an age, they all heard a car pull up outside. It was getting dark, and the cicadas had begun their nightly serenade. The captives could hear muffled voices and then the sound of a man's voice shouting,

"You should've got rid of them all! Now they will know my plans, idiot, you've ruined everything!" Maria looked worried, suddenly torn between helping her brother and keeping a watch on her captives.

"Now get on with your job Miguel, I'll deal with you later."

An older man entered the barn.

"Stay where you are Maria, he doesn't need you." He barked.

A look passed over Maria's face that could turn a person to stone, that look was gone almost as soon as it appeared, Armando had seen it and it chilled him to the bone. It was a look devoid of all feelings apart from hate.

The man that stood before them was at least 65. He was impeccably dressed and was of average height, his hair was greying at the edges, his face was almost unlined, and Armando thought something about it didn't look natural. It was his eyes that struck Armando as extraordinary. They seemed to look straight through you. They were blue, no laughter lines surrounded them. He looked cruel, his face was that of a man used to getting his own way and using any method to get it.

"You see, I want to retire to this farm and raise horses. I feel I'm owed it as I once wanted to marry a girl from here, but she ran away. I will have it! I cannot allow you, any of you, to spoil my plans."

Joe looked shocked; he knew the farm belonged to him. He suddenly realised that this might be the man his mother had run away from Spain to avoid. "And now he wants to raise horses, "Huh.``He thought "Not blooming likely." He began to shuffle his feet on the floor beneath him, he grew more and more angry at the thought that this farm would be stolen by this man. If he was the man his mother had run from then he must be bad. She'd never told Joe what he'd done. But he'd been able to see she had been disgusted by this person.

"Maria, see they do not leave here." With that the man turned on his heel and walked out.

They heard a car engine start and screech away from the yard at speed. Armando and Karim exchanged a glance. Armando worked away at the bonds, trying to loosen the knots that tied him to the beam. They had been tied well and left little room for manoeuvre. He noticed Joe shuffling his feet and thought that he must be nervous. He saw that Karim was also trying to break free.

"Your boss didn't seem too pleased with you Maria, finally messed up, have you?" Armando goaded her,

"I'll bet he doesn't keep you on after this, you and your brother will be marked for disposal."

"Not as soon as you Officer, you'll soon be going to another place!"

Her eyes had a wildness as if she were excited by the prospect of the violence to come, Armando could see she revelled in it, inhaling the toxic atmosphere.

"You know in Suffolk, we build barns better than this, they last for centuries." Joe broke in. "The one on my farm was built in the 16th Century, made of pure English oak of course, much better than this construction. I mean look at it. The roof is made of corrugated iron sheets for goodness' sake! You can see the wind whistling through the boards on the side of the barn, termites everywhere and dry rot, no doubt. One good gust of wind and the whole place would fall. No good for your animals I can tell you. Pigs like to be warm and dry. I'll have to rebuild when I move in"

Maria looked mystified and turned her gun on Joe, "Shut up English man! You're crazy, I'm going to kill all of you, and you are talking about barns, you will never live here. Never! Neither will your precious pigs. You will only get a hole in the ground. "She strode over to Antonia and began to untie her. "Come, ladies first."

Joe had been looking at the roof of the barn as he talked. Maria was engrossed in untying Antonia. His feet shuffled at the earth at the bottom of the beam then he shouted.

"Oh! my stomach, Oh God, I think I'm going to throw up."

He crouched down as far as he could with his arms tied behind him.

"Get up!" screamed Maria, leaving Antonia to move in front of Joe. "Get up now!"

Joe steadied one shoulder against the beam, placed his back foot firmly into the floor of the barn then gave the beam an almighty shove with his back. There was a loud crack and the beam started to fall backwards loosening Joe's bonds and destroying the support for the corrugated sheeting.

Quick as a flash Joe wriggled to the open end of the beam and freed himself, leaping out of the way as over his head the heavy corrugated iron sheeting toppled rapidly. Maria watched as it fell and jumped back, though not far enough, the edge of the sheet neatly sliced through her gun holding shoulder almost severing her arm and causing the gun to fire rapidly at the roof bringing down more debris.

She screamed as the sheet pinned her underneath it's considerable weight. Joe ran and picked up Maria's gun. He quickly checked the door to make sure no one else had appeared, then ran to Armando and released him.

"Here," he said as he handed the gun over" I'm sure you are better with this than I am."

"Neat move" said Armando "making the beam collapse like that, you are stronger than you look."

"Termites" was all Joe said in reply.

Miguel was dealing with Bob Last, whom he had found waiting outside the fence. He heard the sound of gunfire and shoved Bob roughly into the boot of a car and shut the lid then ran back towards the barn.

"Go and free Karim and Antonia, Joe. I'll watch for the other evil twin." Armando headed for the door of the barn as Joe released Antonia and Karim.

"Stay here." said Karim as he headed for the door

Miguel ran around the house towards the barn. His knife was in his left hand like a trusted friend, he crossed the yard in time to see Armando emerge from the barn.

Miguel threw his knife, it flew ahead of him catching the light as it spun, almost in the same instant Armando aimed his gun and pressed the trigger, he felt the recoil just as the knife hit him. He felt the tip of the knife pierce through the flesh of his chest and firmly embed itself in the hollow under his collarbone. He stumbled back as the pain hit him but managed to stay on his feet, looking across he saw shock registering on Miguel's face, his hand feeling the bullet wounds before finally staggering and falling face first to lie motionless on the dry earth. Karim ran to Armando,

"Are you OK boss?" He helped Armando sit down.

"Here press the edges of the wound with your hand, don't take that knife out, there could be more damage on the inside."

"Yes Karim, I have done the emergency first aid course. Thanks."

Karim gave him a look that said "Really?" Then phoned for an ambulance for Armando and Antonia, who was in shock.· Then he phoned Elena and asked her to come to the scene. It was fully dark now and the cicadas were singing in the night air. The midnight blue sky was clear and full of stars. The air was cooler, but the temperature was still warm.

Joe and Antonia joined Armando in the yard, Antonia fussed over Armando and Joe looked distastefully at

Miguel's body. He found an old sack in the doorway of the barn and used it to cover Miguel. Maria was dead, the corrugated iron had severed an artery in her arm, and she now lay in a pool of her own blood on the floor.

Antonia was still quite shaken, and a bruise was beginning to show itself on her cheek. Joe paced up and down, his anger at what had happened had not quite abated and his stomach still hurt from the punch Miguel had delivered.

"Why has this happened?" Joe asked

"It is a long story, Mr Odreck, but, needless to say, your actions have saved us all. I didn't think that barn was so fragile. It's a good job you know about termites! We have a job to finish now and get rid of Senor Cabanillos for the last time. Then we can meet, and I will explain everything."

They heard cars pull up and the dog began barking once more as Elena and Jorge and the paramedic came through the gate. Elena ran to Armando, concern furrowing her brow. "What happened? Here let me see."

"I'm OK Elena, look, the paramedic is going to take good care of me."

"That wound is quite deep, detective, I'll do what I can, but you will need to come to the hospital. It will have to be stitched, don't move it too much. This sling will help you keep it still."

"If anything had happened to you Armando…" she said. "Don't you think it is about time you took me to dinner?"

Armando smiled despite the pain in his shoulder.

"Yes Elena, I have been meaning to ask you for such a long time, stupid really."

Elena smiled.

Jorge checked that Karim and Antonia were all right, Antonia was still uttering a stream of very un-lady-like Spanish expletives under her breath. Joe held her hand and tried to calm her down. Jorge looked at Joe, he seemed very caring. Jorge was further impressed when he heard about Joe and the collapsing roof. Joe looked up and caught Jorge looking at him. Their eyes met and Joe felt that, possibly, something passed between them.

"Hello" he said, "I'm Joe Odreck." Jorge extended his hand which Joe grasped.

"I'm Jorge Rodriguez, Assistant to forensic officer Elena."

"Pleased to meet you Jorge" Joe smiled. They stood motionless, hands joined for a while until Joe suddenly felt awkward and stepped back.

"How long will you be in Malaga Joe?" Jorge asked

"I still have some things to sort out here at my farm." Joe replied

"Your…?"

"Yes, I can't believe it myself yet, but this belongs to me. It was my great grandfather's. He left it to me."

"Good to meet you, Joe. I wonder…" Jorge was cut off mid-sentence.

"Hey Jorge!" Elena shouted. "Come on, we've got work to do!"

"Sorry Joe, I've got to go." He turned to join Elena

Chapter 34

Armando suddenly remembered Inspector Last.

"Karim find Bob. I hope he's still alive."

Karim went off in search of Inspector Last. Armando sat with Antonia and Joe while Elena started her meticulous work of photographing the scene and inspecting the bodies.

Karim skirted around the guard dog; he had never liked dogs since being bitten as a child. Its saliva filled mouth made Karim shudder.

He called Bob's name several times and at last heard a faint shouting and banging coming from the boot of an old car. He cautiously opened the boot and saw Bob, laying on his side. He had a bruise on the side of his forehead circling a break in the skin with blood trailing away from it across his face. Karim freed the ropes that tied him and hauled Bob from the boot.

"Thanks Karim, I thought I was a gonner for sure." He groaned as he straightened up, still feeling a little hot and dizzy.

"The boss, Cabanillos, has been here, there was a fight after he left and his henchmen are dead, Armando is injured. We still have work to do. The drug shipment must be stopped, and we must catch Rafael Cabanillos."

"Well, let's get on with it then." Bob said

Later, back at police headquarters Armando desperately wanted to sit down. His shoulder was hurting badly, and the painkillers the hospital had given him were wearing off. The officer at the desk, seeing his pale complexion, asked if he needed a chair but Armando said no, he would sit in his office.

Armando needed some time to gather his thoughts and write a report on the day's events. Before the trip to the farm, He had managed to return Senora Gomez's call and she had told him what she knew about Rafael Cabanillos. He knew he was a criminal but now had a fuller picture of his brutality. He had sent Dominguez to pick up a photograph of Rafael in his younger years and this was now pinned to the wall of the incident room. He wanted to be ready for the team on Saturday morning. It was well past midnight when he stood up, flinching at the pain in his shoulder, noticing the blood was seeping through the dressing. He knew he should go back to the hospital but the shipment from the factory was supposed to take place and he intended to be there and close this case finally.

Chapter 35

Saturday morning and Armando's team were ready and waiting when he arrived at headquarters. The incident room buzzed with anticipation and the aroma of strong coffee as each member of the team prepared themselves for action. Karim balanced on the edge of the cabinets that lined the side wall of the office opposite the frosted window. He hardly ever sat still in a chair and was a picture of pent-up energy ready to move at any moment.

A sickly pot plant perched at the other end of the cabinets miserably failing in its mission to brighten up the room. Karim was the only one who had escaped without a scratch after yesterday's incident. Armando's shoulder was bandaged, Bob sported a black eye, but they were all faring better than Maria and Miguel who lay in the pathologist's chiller waiting for Elena.

"We know now that Rafael Cabanillos is the boss, now we know he is working with the Russians on the drug shipments. Karim got every bit of information he could. That together with the information from Senora Gomez, means we know that we are dealing with a vicious and sadistic criminal. Yesterday's incident at the farm has at least removed that pair Maria and Miguel from the scene. We must proceed with caution and above all make sure he does not escape."

Bob Last sat on the chair to the right of Armando, despite having slept well he had been woken by the noisy street cleaners banging the dumpsters beneath his room and shouting to each other in what he assumed was Spanish banter.

"Some things are the same wherever you go in the world." he thought.

He had looked at his watch and found it was five thirty. He'd showered and dressed then and made his way out of the hotel to take a walk around the block and mull over all that had happened. He couldn't get the thought of Maisie out of his head. He had known her since she joined the force and hoped he had helped her in her career. She was a good officer, one of the best. She should have gone to the top, not be lying on a slab in the mortuary.

By the time he'd returned from his walk he'd felt his anger building, he wanted to see the man responsible brought to justice even if he had to mete that out himself. He must join his Spanish colleagues on the raid. He wouldn't let Armando talk him out of it.

"Bugger the rules!" he'd said as he'd walked past some locals who gave him a very strange look.

The Head of the Serious Crime Squad sat opposite Bob Last. Mateo De la Fuente had been in the police force since leaving college and now at fifty-six he was looking forward to retirement. His long-suffering wife, Isabella and his 6 children had waited for him all those years, all through the missed birthdays, weddings and even holidays. It was time that he paid them back for their patience. He was finishing work in three months and could not wait.

Elena sat in the chair next to Armando's. She looked refreshed after only a few hours rest, the bruising on her head fading to a pale green. She was more than ready to give her professional report of all the evidence she had found. At the end of the table sat Officer Dominguez. Armando had asked him to come so that he could take a report back to the local office. He did not believe in operating separately from the Local police as their local knowledge was invaluable. Dominguez wouldn't be on the raid but was there to listen.

Armando's boss, Martin Jerez, sat at the back of the room. He was an observer and would organise the extra resource of ten officers that would be deployed under Armando's command. But that morning he had received a call instructing him to call off the raid. If he did not his family would suffer. He had phoned his wife at home and told her to go immediately to Burgos, to visit relatives, his wife had understood the urgency and hurried the children out of the house.

It was a risk, he knew but if all went well, the raid would put an end to Rafael Cabanillos and that meant that he and his family would be safe. Maybe he could even retire.

Chapter 36

Rafael was driving towards Malaga, he had not heard from Miguel or Maria and assumed they had dealt with the problems at the farm and would be at the factory tonight as planned. They had never let him down before, so he was confident that all would go well. He had been successful in all his activities over the years, his private life was another matter. He had one regret and that was he did not have a son to pass his empire on to. The first stupid girl he had wanted to marry had run away to England just because he had slapped her when she wouldn't do what she was asked. He had made her obey him. He savoured the thought of her in the forest that day. Her grandparents had had the farm and that was his main reason for courting the girl in the first place. He wanted the farm and the land even then.

The next one, Marguerite had been a bigger disappointment, first by not having his child and then she did not immediately bend to his will. He had beaten her into submission, as all husbands would if they were not such cowards, he would never let a woman rule him!

She was ungrateful for all the things he gave her and had run off one night. He knew she lived in Nerja and as soon as this business was over, he would make sure he found her and punished her for her treachery. He could not let her get away with it, even after all this time. Rafael grew excited at the thought of punishing Marguerite. He felt power surge through him as he always did when he pictured Marguerite prostrate on the floor in front of him begging for mercy. He would have dealt with her sooner but a businessman's life such as his, didn't leave time for the type of revenge he had planned. A surprise reunion and a private party at her house and then a short walk to a high cliff near the Carabeo and she would be gone.

Chapter 37

"Karim, can you tell us what you know about this man, Rafael Cabanillos." Armando sat and let Karim take the floor.

"Rafael has never been arrested since 1969 when he was caught for a minor fight in a bar in Nerja, the picture we have is old, but undoubtedly this is the same man that was at the barn, in charge of the twins."

Karim projected the picture of a young man, looking straight at the camera obviously not happy to be there, His cold staring eyes bored into the camera.

"He has several businesses both here and in the UK. He also owns the Iberico ham factory outside Malaga. He exports goods to the UK and other parts of Europe." Karim continued

"But there are no further arrests. His picture does not appear on any social media sites or business magazines, he is very careful not to be photographed. Several women have come forward to report him over the years for assault, but they always mysteriously disappear or withdraw the charges, before they can testify in court."

"Drug dealing is just one of his lines of business," Finished Karim.

"Inspector Last do you have anything to add? "Asked Armando

"We found a shipment of ham from the factory in Malaga in Ipswich. The ham joints each contained a quantity of cocaine amounting to about 200kg.

I allowed Maisie Bright time off, not to pursue this, but because she had suffered an injury in an incident, and I thought this was the reason she needed a leave of absence. I thought Constable Bright was on holiday. It's true that after the death of her brother she was a little overwrought. I had no idea she was in Malaga by herself. Her brother died of a drug overdose. She had wanted to join the drug squad, but I didn't feel she was ready. The business with her brother had made her too obsessive and it was starting to affect her job."

"Thanks Inspector Last." Armando continued

"I think we should look out for associates of this Yasha the Basher, the Russian, and be prepared for them to put up a fight." Said Armando.

"Mateo what have you got for us?"

Mateo sat forward. "I have my squad and ten other officers are under your command Armando. The Russians consist of six men according to our surveillance, they seem to be unloading and loading goods at the far-right hand side of the loading bay. We should be able to disarm them and the vehicle driver and confiscate the goods."

The Boss, Martin Jerez, nodded his head as a signal for Armando to continue. Armando switched the slide to the floor plans of the factory.

"There is an entrance off the main road for lorries to get in. There are bays for at least 15 lorries to pull in. We are dealing with bays 14 and 15 at the far end. There is a small pedestrian entrance beside this. The building has two floors. Upstairs are the offices; a fire exit comes from there to the other side of the loading bay. In the factory there is the processing and packaging plant, the packaging plant is nearest to the loading bay. There are two more fire exits that need to be manned at the opposite side of the building. We need to make sure no-one gets out of the building. We also need to catch Rafael Cabanillos and bring him to justice.

Mateo, you know where best to station your men, mine will be at the fire exits and gates to the factory. Karim will go with your team into the building. I will follow Senor Cabanillos, he must be caught at the scene. We don't have a lot to connect him with the drug running at present, so it is vital he is caught red handed. I also owe him for the attack on Elena."

"Officer Dominguez, do you have anything to add?"

Pedro Dominguez sat up. "I was talking to some of the local bar owners near the Carabeo and some had seen Senor Cabanillos in the Parador Hotel, I checked with the receptionist and after some persuasion he confirmed that Cabanillos is staying there. The owner of the fruit and vegetable shop on the Carabeo also said he saw him watching Senora Gomez's house. I have asked her to stay with her friend Berta Molinera until this is all over. "

"Good work Officer." Said Armando "Now we know where he is staying, I will put someone there to see if he returns to the hotel this afternoon and follow him. They can keep me updated."

"When we arrest Rafael Cabanillos, I think we should also question him about the death of Juan Molinera, the security guard who "fell" into the machinery at the factory. Knowing what we know, is it possible that he saw something he shouldn't have?" Karim asked.

"Good idea, Karim. Dominguez, I may have some more work for you investigating that."

Pedro Dominguez sat a little straighter in his chair. Pleased to be included.

Elena then gave the team the details about where the cocaine was hidden in the ham joints and what to look out for.

"No testing the cocaine with your tongues please, we will leave that to Hollywood. It is inaccurate and dangerous. This is grade one pure cocaine, ready for the dealers to cut with other substances. worth about 40 Euros per gram"

When all the details had been hashed out the team took a break and made final preparations for the raid. With good planning and a little luck, it would go well. They would meet in a quiet street near the factory at 10:00 PM. The shipment was due out sometime after midnight "We must stop it and arrest all the criminals involved. I know I have the best team so let's get it right." Armando stood and wished everyone luck.

Elena stayed behind until everyone had gone.

"Be careful Armando, remember we have a date." She said holding his hand.

She was suddenly terrified that something would happen to him. He pulled her to him and looked down into her blue eyes.

"Don't worry Elena, nothing will stop me taking you out. I'm only sorry I didn't have the courage to ask you before now." He kissed her then and held her in his arms. He had never had to worry about anyone but himself before but now felt responsible for Elena as well as his team. There was definitely more at stake.

At 22:00 hours, Armando and Karim met the rest of the team and after finalising the details, They checked their service revolvers, radios and torches. they synchronised their watches and got into position.

Chapter 38

Before moving off Armando reminded them.

"No radio contact until we are ready to engage, they may be monitoring police radios in the area."

"Yes Boss" came the reply.

Bob Last was there, and although Armando had given him strict instructions to stay out of the way he watched them as they moved off. He was damned if they thought he was going to wait around outside like a naughty schoolboy. After a couple of minutes, he followed the team inside.

Mateo was ready, his men entered the compound, keeping close to the wall and proceeded to head for the loading bay. They were experts and confident in their role of securing the area. As they approached the storage area leading to the bay, Mateo saw the shadow of someone running down the aisle of crates ahead of them then gunfire erupted. Ducking for cover his men tried to see where the shooter was. Mateo signalled to the right and fired three shots in rapid succession. The shooter fell from behind some crates and lay still. The squad moved on, more cautious now, aware that their presence was no longer a secret.

Karim, together with a drugs squad officer, had headed straight for the loading bay via the outside of the building. They could see four men moving boxes into the loading area. When the men heard gunfire from inside the factory, they drew their weapons and positioned themselves to defend the cargo.

"You take the two on the left and I will deal with the other two" Karim whispered to the Officer from the Drug team. Karim fired 4 rounds in rapid succession and the four in the loading bay dropped to the floor and lay still. He looked over at his colleague and shrugged

"Too slow old man!"

The Officer grinned and got ready to move on.

Just as they were about to move a fifth man appeared, it was Rafael Cabanillos, Armando had heard nothing from the officer who was watching out for him in Nerja. He must have missed him, Rafael was in the building already.

Rafael had come to investigate the crates and make sure all was well when he heard the gunfire and saw his men motionless, he began to panic. He ran into the processing plant. Armando was off like a bullet after Rafael.

As Karim was passing one of the packing cases, one of the injured Russian men raised his arm and shot at Karim, he felt the bullet rip through his calf. As he fell, he returned fire, killing his assailant. His leg was bleeding heavily, and he knew he could not go on. He was worried that Armando would be outnumbered. Bob Last suddenly appeared beside him. He took off his tie and made a makeshift tourniquet for Karim's leg, then calling for medical back up he took Karim's gun and ran after Armando.

Armando followed Rafael to the factory processing floor. The lights were off, and he could hear Rafael's footsteps in the distance. A shot rang out ricocheting past Armando's head. Armando ducked behind the conveyer belt and looked carefully out. He could not see Rafael but just beside his arm the switch for the conveyer and the packing machine jutted out. Armando hit the button and the machinery started up, it was noisy, and Armando hoped it would cover the sound of his pursuit and make Rafael disorientated.

Bob Last had just entered the same area, following the noise and saw Armando in front of him. He found the light switches and the factory was flooded with light. He could see Rafael shielding his eyes. Taking aim with Karim's gun he took a shot at Rafael. He missed and Rafael ran up a short flight of metal steps that led to a walkway above the conveyer. Rafael tried to find the best angle to take Armando out, but his view was obscured by the joints of pork. Armando leaned out and saw Rafael's shoulder just above him. He fired a shot which missed,

"Damn."

He quickly followed the path taken by Rafael, but when he reached the top of the walkway Rafael had disappeared through the fire exit at the bottom of some metal steps. He was sure this exit had not been on the plans of the factory.

Armando pushed through the fire exit door in time to see a car accelerate towards the factory gate. Armando followed, radioing Karim.

"Everything OK there Karim?" he asked, "I'm following Cabanillos, he has managed to get away in his car."

"One of these guys in the loading bay is still alive. I have been shot but I'm sitting on his chest at the moment." Karim said. "I'm learning some great Russian swear words even though my leg is killing me. I'll be fine, get after him Armando, don't let him disappear. "

"Sit tight. Mateo should be with you soon."

Armando ran to his car, jumped in and sped through the factory gates, he thought he could see Rafael's brake lights in the distance,

"He must be travelling at some speed to be that far ahead." thought Armando.

He kept following the flashing red lights, the road was uneven and winding. Then Armando lost him, he drove round a bend and nothing…There were several small tracks off the main road and miles of industrial units and green houses. Armando reversed and drove slowly up and down the tracks. Next, he turned off his engine and listened carefully for the sound of another vehicle, but nothing came.

"Where could he have gone?" Armando slammed the steering wheel with frustration and suddenly Marguerite Gomez came to mind. Would Cabanillos be mad enough to try and exact his revenge on her now? If he did, he really was insane and would surely be caught. Armando thought of the tale that Senora Gomez had told him and knew that that was exactly what Rafael planned. He restarted the engine and sped towards Nerja.

It was one of those nights on the coast when the mist rolled in off the ocean, covering the land in a soft blanket of grey. Rafael drove fast, he knew the roads and was confident he would be able to get to Marguerite before that cop.

Rafael couldn't believe it had all gone so wrong but vowed that this last act of his would be perfect. Then he would disappear. Over the years he had salted away a lot of money in various offshore accounts. They were not in his own name of course but one of his many pseudonyms. South Africa appealed to him, the climate was warm, or maybe Malaysia where life was cheap and there were plenty of opportunities for making money.

Chapter 39

Elena arrived to start the forensic investigation. Mateo found four crates of Ham joints laced with cocaine ready for shipment. If her previous find was anything to go by that amounted to at least 200kg of cocaine.

"Great Mateo, that will stop the supply for a while. I'm glad you and your team had no casualties." said Karim as he shook his hand firmly. "With this one under arrest we may be able to trace the Russian connection."

"I will retire in three weeks. It would be good if I could end my career on a high."

Chapter 40

Marguerite looked out of her window onto the street and saw Officer Dominguez was still at his post. It was very comforting to know she had protection. She returned to her bed and took up her novel "La Ruta Infinita." About Magellan's adventures circumnavigating the globe. She soon felt her eyes close and fell into a deep sleep. She didn't hear a thing as Dominguez fell to the floor outside nor did she hear the door being forced open letting in the cool night air nor the footsteps ascending the stairs.

Rafael took his time, his breath stilled as he felt the powerful anticipation of what was to come. He had been patient, but he had always promised himself that he would take his revenge on Marguerite. He turned the handle of the door in front of him and saw Marguerite's sleeping form in the bed. He crossed the room and leaned over her, gripping her wrist roughly he snarled

"Hello bitch!"

That voice woke her, she knew it well, Marguerite knew he had come for her. She began to shake, too frightened to move.

"How nice to see you at last, you ran away from me. Did you think I didn't know where you were? I am going to have to punish you, you know that don't you?"

He stood beside the bed and Marguerite drew her feet up away from him, making herself as small as possible and twisting her arm to try and free it from his grip. She looked round desperately for something to defend herself. She didn't understand how he had managed to get in. Dominguez was outside, wasn't he?

"You see there is no escape from me. You are mine until I decide to get rid of you, you don't decide that! Only me."

His voice was soft and low, and Marguerite knew that was when he was at his most dangerous.

"Why? You don't need me." She stuttered

"Because you belong to me Puta! You are mine, I will always be inside your head, I decide, not you."

With that he pulled her from the bed, her head banged painfully on the floor, and she tried to kick out at him, but he was too strong and punched her in the ribs which took her breath away. He dragged her to the small balcony off her bedroom and tore her night clothes using the satin belt to tie her arms to the railing.

"Now sit there whore and wait."

Marguerite remembered this is what he used to do to her. Making her wait, terrified of his return. It was happening again, she was terrified even after all these years.

She heard him rifling through her belongings and when he returned, he held her jewellery in his fist. "I deserve these" he smirked "It's payment for the inconvenience of having to come after you."

Marguerite tried to struggle with her ties, but Rafael hit her with the jewellery bunched in his fist and she felt her lip split and warm blood trickle down her chin. Her head swam, the house next door was empty, it was a holiday let so no one would hear.

Rafael looked over the balcony, "Quite a drop, isn't it? I'm sure no one could survive that fall. Especially a nervous lonely old woman! Come on, up we go."

Rafael grabbed Marguerite's hair and pulled her to her feet.

"I should have done this years ago, but I allowed you to live. Say Gracias Rafael."

Marguerite stayed silent. She would not speak again. Rafael drew back his fist and hit her in the stomach, she retched and leaned forward. He untied her and again he held her upright. He pinned her against the wall and the railing and turned her, so she was facing the sea.

"How beautiful it looks." Thought Marguerite, "It will be good to be free of him at last."

Rafael felt the thrill of his power over her and suddenly kissed her shoulder, she flinched at his touch as he bit her hard. She screamed and struggled against him as she felt him undo his flies and kick her legs apart." Marguerite pushed back violently the back of her head colliding with his face. He gasped and stepped back ready to attack again, he grabbed her more firmly and pressed his body into hers, pinning her against the railing he kicked her legs apart once more and held her neck, twisting it violently to the side. Marguerite's mind went blank, she felt her vision fading. A loud bang exploded by her ear, she was disorientated but felt Rafael loosen his grip and turn away from her, she sank to her knees, and she heard two more loud bangs, then she saw Rafael stumble backwards, his hand released her and grasped for the railing instead. His weight carried him over the top and onto the rocks below.

Armando ran to Marguerite who was still cowering on the balcony.

"It's O.K. Marguerite, he's gone" he said softly "He can't hurt you anymore."

He lifted Marguerite and carried her to the bed and placed her down gently. She was still in shock and shivered.

Armando lifted the covers over her and rang for an ambulance.

He had found Dominguez outside, unconscious with a nasty gash on the side of his head and after checking his breathing and placing him on his side he had run into Marguerite's house and up the stairs to see that Cabanillos was attacking her. There was no time for a warning. Armando knew that any hesitation on his part would have led to Marguerite's death and so he had fired. He knew his shot would find its mark, he never missed a target.

Chapter 41

At 6 am on Sunday Morning the team arrived back at headquarters. Armando spent the rest of the day writing up reports, bolstered by drinking plenty of black coffee. He noted down everything about the raid and all that had happened previously. Bob Last rang his commander in Suffolk and gave him the information he needed to tie up the UK end of the operation. Yasha the Basher was talking nonstop, hoping to get a lighter sentence. With the information the lorry driver had given after his arrest, they were able to raid the distribution point in Suffolk and arrest the main culprits in the UK.

Elena returned to her lab and met Maisie Bright's mother so that she could identify her daughter and take her home. It was the worst part of her job, but she was glad that they had caught the killer and his boss, and that Armando was OK.

Poor Karim was not so lucky. His wounded leg needed treatment. However, Elena was sure that he would revel in the attention.

Elena looked up from her desk at 17:00 thinking that she would be able to go home soon and was surprised to see Armando at her door. He crossed the office quickly and took her in his arms.

"Let's go home." he said

"Home?"

"Yes, Home, I have some unfinished business there before taking a gorgeous woman out to dinner"

"Who is this woman? Do I know her?"

Armando kissed her and lifted her off her feet.

"It is you Elena, only you."

Joe sat with Antonia Munoz, and they talked over the developments of the last few days. Joe was still amazed that he had found his home in Spain. It had all been a bit of a whirlwind. He didn't feel that he had really taken it all in, but he did know that he wanted to live in Spain and bring his pigs with him to the new farm.

"That paperwork will give Bill a headache!" He thought.

He would farm in the Spanish hills. develop a new breed of pig and be happy in the sun. The roof would still leak, most likely, and that barn would need some rebuilding but the sale of the farm in Suffolk would raise some capital. He felt closer to his roots here and looked forward to a brighter future. Questions remained, about whether his mother and Rafael Cabanillos had been involved with each other long ago, but they were now unanswerable. If the criminal had been his father, Joe didn't really want to know. What he did however want to know more about, if he could, was Jorge...

Chapter 42

The Chief of Police Martin Perez, sat in his office. Rafael's death had meant he was off the hook, but he couldn't be sure he was safe as Rafael's associates were still in the background and he didn't know how much they knew of his involvement. For the moment he would breathe but keep looking over his shoulder. Sitting back in his chair in the office he thought about how the whole thing had started.

He met Rafael Cabanillos about a year after qualifying at the Police Academy. He had been a young brash policeman, eager to make his mark. Rafael had appeared to be an honest businessman after a while they became friends and often had coffee together when Martin was in Malaga. So, when Martin Perez got into some difficulty with a local casino, gambling had always been his downfall, he had turned to the only person he thought would be able to help him. One day he was patrolling the streets and Raphael had approached him to ask for his loan back. Martin did not have that amount and so Rafael had asked him to pay back some of the debt with a favour. It was not much, just to lose some evidence held in the police store. To his later regret Martin had done what he was asked and from that moment on Rafael demanded more and more.

Marguerite Gomez and Berta Molinera sat in the shade of the orange trees outside Café Ani, sipping their afternoon coffee and enjoying a sweet biscuit.

"Well Marguerite, you are safe from that tyrant at last." said Berta

"Yes, and because you know that Jose's death was not an accident you can get some compensation."

Rafael's people had spoken to the police rather more readily than anyone had imagined. Jose had started to get too close to the truth when they had killed him.

"I would rather have Jose back. I'm still so lonely without him." said Berta sadly.

"I can't believe that man caused us so much grief, I can stop looking over my shoulder and you can live more comfortably." Marguerite looked around the tranquil terrace and breathed freely at last. Free of her brutal husband and free to live her life without fear. She smiled to herself thankful for the company of her good friend.

The sun dripped fat and lazy on the rooftops of the small Spanish town of Nerja. Some inhabitants fled into the dry dimly lit shade to escape the heat and take solace in a cool cerveza. Others leapt into the soaring oven of heat to lay corpse-like on striped beach towels and be cooked by the sun's rays. The old people of the town kept to their routines: cleaning, shopping, soothing crying grandchildren or sitting bird-like on one of the many benches with their amigos pecking over the news, retreating inside for lunch once the day's heat had reached its peak as the town quietened in the lazy hush of the old-fashioned siesta

End

Printed in Great Britain
by Amazon